HAMSTER IN A HANDBASKET

Mandy caught James's eye. "Can I guess what you're thinking?"

"I'm thinking fresh vegetables, dried oats, nuts, and bread!"

"No more chips?" She began to smile. "James, you're planning to put Henry on a diet!"

"A calorie count," he confirmed.

"A strict diet."

"An exercise plan, so we can bring him back in September looking like a new hamster. No more excess fat." He grinned.

"Poor Henry." Mandy shook her head. "I suppose it's for his own good, though."

"Poor Henry, nothing! My house is going to be the first hamster health farm in the country!"

Give someone you love a home!
Read about the animals of Animal Ark™

HAMSTER in a HANDBASKET

Ben M. Baglio

Illustrations by Shelagh McNicholas

Cover illustration by
Mary Ann Lasher

AN
APPLE
PAPERBACK

SCHOLASTIC INC.
New York Toronto London Auckland Sydney
Mexico City New Delhi Hong Kong

No part of this publication may be reproduced in whole or in part, or stored in a retrieval system, or transmitted in any form or by any means, electronic, mechanical, photocopying, recording, or otherwise, without written permission of the publisher. For information regarding permission, write to Working Partners Limited, 11A Dunraven Road, London W12 7QY, United Kingdom.

ISBN 0-439-09701-0

Text copyright © 1996 by Working Partners Limited.
Original series created by Ben M. Baglio.
Illustrations copyright © 1996 by Shelagh McNicholas.

All rights reserved. Published by Scholastic Inc., 555 Broadway, New York, NY 10012, by arrangement with Working Partners Limited. ANIMAL ARK is a trademark of Working Partners Limited. SCHOLASTIC, APPLE PAPERBACKS, and associated logos are trademarks and/or registered trademarks of Scholastic Inc.

12 11   3 4 5/0

Printed in the U.S.A.   40
First Scholastic printing, May 2000

Special thanks to Jenny Oldfield.
Thanks also to C. J. Hall, B.Vet.Med., M.R.C.V.S.,
for reviewing
the veterinary information contained
in this book.

TM

One

Mandy Hope sat with her chin cupped in both hands. She was daydreaming in class, while sun streamed in through the biology lab window. Miss Temple was handing back the homework books. Mandy gazed at Henry the Eighth, the school hamster, running steadily inside his exercise wheel.

Henry the Eighth was a good name, she decided. Like all hamsters, Henry had a funny habit of pouching his food in his cheeks, which puffed out, making him look enormously fat and self-important. His golden brown whiskers and the flash of white on the chest completed his resemblance to the famous king of England.

1

Treadle-treadle-rattle-spin went the wheel. Henry's squat little legs trotted on. Mandy smiled absentmindedly. Henry was the eighth and last hamster in his litter, hence his name. Miss Temple had found homes for all the rest but had decided to keep Henry as the school pet. She said he was a hamster with attitude. Mandy supposed this meant that he had a glint in his enormous dark eyes. Anyway, Henry had turned into one of the friendliest little animals, happy to sit in your hand nibbling dry oatmeal or to take a small chunk of brown bread and hold it delicately between his front paws.

And that was the problem; he was too friendly and too greedy. Everyone who came up to his cage for a chat slipped him a few goodies. He gobbled chips, sandwich crusts, apple cores. You name it, Henry ate it. And he was fat!

He had a nice life, though, sitting inside his airy wooden cage on the sunniest ledge in the biology lab, alongside the geraniums and the spider plants. He'd put on weight, and no amount of running on the exercise wheel seemed to take it off again. Pudgy, pouchy, overweight little Henry weighed in at a mighty five and a half ounces. He was a heavyweight hamster. Mandy smiled and dreamed on.

"Mandy Hope." Miss Temple's voice brought her back

to earth. "Hello, Mandy. Knock, knock, is anybody there?" She came up to Mandy's seat and rattled her knuckles against it, exercise book at the ready. "Don't you want to know your homework grade?"

Mandy blushed and pushed her blond hair behind her ears. "Sorry." Sheepishly she took her book.

"Don't worry. Only one more day to go before vacation!" Miss Temple's smile was warm and friendly. "You're not the only one who can't wait for the end of the semester."

This time Mandy grinned. She liked the biology teacher, and this wasn't just because biology was her favorite school subject, with all the fascinating facts about animals. Miss Temple herself was bright and young; quite strict when she wanted her pupils to pay attention, but open to a joke and a kind word. She didn't look like a teacher, either, with her wavy brown hair straying out of its ponytail, and her light summer dresses.

"I was watching Henry doing his workout," Mandy explained.

Miss Temple glanced at her watch and told the class to pack away their things. "Ah, our dear little *Mesocricetus auratus*! That's his official, scientific name." She smiled, glancing at Henry. "Or not so little, as the case may be. He could really do with being put on a strict diet. And that reminds me." She walked back to the front of the class and clapped her hands for attention. "Listen for a moment, everyone!"

Mandy watched a couple of people in the front row whispering and giggling behind their hands. End-of-the-year fever was really setting in. One girl, Vicki Simpson, had turned bright red and sat on the edge of her seat. She watched Miss Temple step up to her desk. Vicki's friend Becky Severn dug her in the ribs and warned her to be quiet. Meanwhile, Vicki's twin brother, Justin, retreated from Miss Temple's desk, a wide grin spread across his round, freckled face.

Miss Temple clapped again and the room fell silent. "I want to make an announcement before the bell rings." She paused and cocked her head to one side. She listened hard. "What's that noise?"

In the silence, Mandy could hear Henry plodding steadily inside his wheel. *Treadle-treadle-rattle-spin.* "It's Henry, Miss Temple!" she volunteered, pointing him out to the teacher.

But Miss Temple frowned. "No, not that. Something else; a kind of whirring sound." She leaned across her desk toward a dust cloth carelessly scrunched and pushed to one side.

Mandy saw Justin's grin expand. Vicki's face was ready to explode into laughter.

Miss Temple peered at the red-checked dust cloth. The faint whirring sound was definitely coming from under there. Gingerly she poked the cloth, then raised a tiny corner. The whirring grew louder, like an angry bee.

Miss Temple gritted her teeth. She lifted the cloth clear of the desk. A round, fat, hairy thing with eight long, spindly legs shot out from under it. Mandy stared wide-eyed. The "thing" was a giant spider; a noisy, buzzing, creeping, hairy-legged spider.

Vicki Simpson jumped to her feet for a better view. Becky held her back. Justin jumped onto his seat. The whole class was in an uproar!

The spider shot across the desk, whirring angrily. It scrabbled across the length of the teacher's desk and came up against a tall pile of textbooks, where it whirred and flailed.

"Hmm." Miss Temple put on her best science teacher's voice. "I suspect it's *Arachnis dunlophobia*, a very rare species indeed." She poked at the spider with the sharp end of a pencil. It turned and sprinted back along the desk. A squeal shivered around the class.

Mandy squinted hard at the creature. Its gray bumpy

body was covered in ugly yellow blotches. It had big red eyes. Its legs, those long, hairy things, moved like clockwork. Ah! She caught Miss Temple's eye. Clockwork, she thought.

"Now, everyone, calm down and stand back. Justin, get down from that chair, please," the biology teacher ordered. She went straight to the high shelf behind her desk and brought back a large, empty glass jar. "I want to take this specimen alive." Swiftly she trapped the spider inside the jar. A muffled whirring emerged. Legs scrambled helplessly against the glass. The spider tumbled and rolled. Then the whirring slowed and faded to a stop.

"Is it dead, Miss Temple?" Justin demanded. He grinned at his twin sister.

Miss Temple winked at Mandy. "No, Justin. *Arachnis dunlophobia* is a tougher species than that!" Carefully she lifted the jar and picked up the spider between thumb and forefinger. "In fact, if we just wind this little knob here, I expect we'll soon revive him, no problem!" She smiled as she wound up the rubbery toy and placed it right-side up on the desk once more. Sure enough, the spider began charging in straight lines up and down the desk.

"Oh!" Becky Severn sat back in her seat and fanned

herself. "It's a trick!" Vicki bit her lip, waiting to see how the teacher would react. Only Justin remained calm. Mandy saw him, standing with his hands in his pockets, the grin fixed on his sturdy face.

Miss Temple raised her eyebrows at him. "What a pity, Justin. I thought we were on to an exciting scientific discovery there. A Nobel prize at the very least."

Justin kept on grinning. But when Miss Temple took the toy spider and placed it, legs still whirring away, inside her drawer, his smile began to fade. "Hey, Miss Temple, that's my spider!" he complained.

She cut him short. "Yes, Justin, I know perfectly well it's *your* spider. But I think I'll just keep an eye on it for the rest of the day, if you don't mind. Now, you can make yourself nice and useful." She picked up the dust cloth and thrust it toward him in a cloud of chalk. "Why don't you clean the board for me while I make my announcement? I'll have a word with you during break, *after* the bell rings."

Justin's mouth turned down, but Miss Temple had the upper hand. She hadn't panicked; she'd turned the joke against him. She waited until Justin settled into his task, then turned to the rest of the class.

Good for you, Mandy thought. Justin was well known as a loudmouth and a bully. But Miss Temple had handled him well. She saw his twin sister sit back in her place, head down, unwilling to make eye contact. Gradually everyone settled down.

"It's about Henry," Miss Temple began. "We need to find him a good home for vacation." A murmur ran around the room. The teacher raised both hands, asking for quiet. "We need someone who can collect the cage after school tomorrow, take it home, and look after him for three months. That means preferably someone whose family is not going on vacation themselves, whom we can rely on to change the wood chips every day and to make sure that Henry gets his exercise and food and a bit of regular company." She paused while people considered this.

Mandy sighed and gazed at Henry. He'd stopped exercising and come out onto the floor of his cage to groom. His lovely marmalade-colored coat shone in the sun. He stared back at her with his nearsighted, twinkling dark eyes. His nose and whiskers twitched. If only, she thought. Looking after Henry for the summer would be fantastic. But it was out of the question. As vets at Animal Ark, her mom and dad had a rule that they would never take in extra animals; not strays, nor friends' cats and dogs, nor orphans from the wild. "We're not a boarding kennel, Mandy. We're vets," her mom would say, kindly but firmly. "No extra responsibilities, remember. We have enough as it is."

Mandy reluctantly admitted that her mom and dad were right never to break their rule.

"This person must take great care to feed Henry his proper diet: cereal, bread, nuts, fruit, and vegetables, and not too many snacks!" Miss Temple paused to make the point about Henry's weight problem, then went on. "There must always be clean drinking water in his cage.

And you must be especially careful to keep it locked tight at night. Nighttime is when pet hamsters get up to their tricks if you let them.

"So it's a responsible job, but if you feel you would like to try looking after Henry, please write your name on a piece of paper as you go out of the lab. I'll take all the names and put them into a hat. The one I draw out will be the lucky caretaker. I plan to have the drawing early tomorrow morning, so please come and check to see if you've been lucky. If you are, you can take Henry home with you tomorrow afternoon."

The end of the class bell rang just as Miss Temple drew to a close. Chairs scraped on the floor, and people picked up their bags and started to file out. Miss Temple took Justin into one corner for a stern word, then let him go. He shuffled out. Mandy sighed again as she noticed five or six people lining up to give Miss Temple their slips of paper, Vicki Simpson and Becky Severn among them. She sidled by toward the door.

"How about you, Mandy?" Miss Temple asked, knowing Mandy's love of animals. She stopped her short.

"Sorry, Miss Temple. I can't."

"Going on vacation?"

Mandy shook her head. "No. It's just that we have enough animals to take care of as it is," she said quietly.

"Ah." Miss Temple nodded. "So you can't manage it?"

Mandy shrugged, but an idea shot into her head as she glanced back at Henry, still preening in the sun. "No," she said, her spirits suddenly lifting. "But I think I know someone who can!"

Two

"James!" Mandy cried. The corridor was crowded with kids, all making their way outside for morning recess. She'd spotted her friend's serious face with its mop of straight brown hair and round glasses. "Wait a second!" She squeezed through the crowd toward him.

He turned and gave her a shy grin. "Hi, Mandy." Then he whispered to a couple of friends to go ahead without him. "Where's the fire?" he asked as Mandy caught up with him at last.

"No fire. But listen to this!" she gasped. Her blue eyes were sparkling. "You know Henry?"

"Henry who?"

"Henry the Eighth."

"Yes, sure. He was the one with six wives, wasn't he? He kept killing them off for some reason." James's eyes, twinkling behind his glasses, showed that he was teasing.

"No, not *that* Henry the Eighth. *Our* Henry, the school Henry! Henry the hamster!"

"Oh, *that* Henry." James folded his arms. "I might have guessed it was an animal that you were so worked up about."

Mandy felt people swarm by, knocking against her with their schoolbags, barging down the corridor, heading for the sunny playground. "I'm not worked up!" she protested. Then she grinned at James. "Okay, then, I am. But listen, I've just had this terrific idea!"

James's brown eyes widened. "Uh-oh!"

She grabbed hold of his elbow. "Miss Temple needs someone to take care of Henry during the school vacation," she said. "Well, of course I'd love to do it, but I can't, as you know, because Mom and Dad have this strict rule about pets, but I thought it would be terrific if *you* could take Henry home! Wouldn't it be great if you had him? I could pop in every now and then to help you look after him. Not that you couldn't manage perfectly well by yourself, I realize, but it would be *terrific* if we both took are of him; if your mom and dad say yes, and if you think it's a good idea, too!"

"Whoa!" James put up both hands to fend Mandy off. "Slow down."

Mandy had only paused for breath. "What's the matter? Don't you want to look after Henry? He's *gorgeous*! He's really, really friendly, and he's got a very interesting personality. Hamsters need company, and I'd be able to come nearly every day to help. It's not as if you'd have to do everything. . . ." Mandy began to slow down. She felt herself go hot and red. Here she was, gushing on, and James was standing calmly in the emptying corridor, arms folded, a smile spreading across his face.

"Just hang on a minute," he said slowly.

"Why? James, you have to make your mind up pretty quickly. Miss Temple is in the lab right this minute asking for volunteers. She's going to mix the names up in a hat and draw one out. She'll have finished and gone off to the staff room if we don't hurry up!" Mandy's enthusiasm seemed to be falling on deaf ears. "Don't you want to put your name on the list?"

James sprang his answer on her. "I already have!"

"What?"

"We had biology first period. Miss Temple asked our class the same thing. I was the first to volunteer."

"To look after Henry?"

James nodded, watching her puzzled face.

Mandy blushed even more furiously.

"Great minds think alike," he told her. "When Miss Temple said that Henry needed a home for the summer, I thought, me and Mandy, quick as a flash!"

They began to walk down the steps toward the playground. "Do you think we'll be lucky?" she wondered. "Henry seems to be pretty popular." She glanced up and through the window at the line of pupils still waiting to give their names to Miss Temple.

James shrugged. "Think positive. There's always a chance that my name will be the one!"

"Okay." She smiled. "So you'll go straight home tonight and ask your mom and dad if it would be all right?" The sun in the sheltered playground was almost hot enough to melt the tarmac. Mandy felt the heat and fanned her face.

James nodded. "Do you want to play a game of tennis after school?"

"If it's not too hot," she agreed.

They made their arrangements to go down to the courts by the riverside. "Do you think they'll say yes?" she asked.

"About Henry?" He nodded. "We already have Blackie and Eric to look after. What's one little extra hamster?"

Mandy smiled. Henry wasn't just any old hamster. She suspected he would be quite a handful. But Mr. and Mrs. Hunter didn't know that. And anyway, there was no point counting your chickens before they were hatched; or your hamster before your name had been drawn out of the hat, she thought.

Mandy stretched out on the patio at the back of the house, letting her snack settle before she cycled down to James's house.

In the background she could hear the sharp barks and muffled yelps of some of the residents in the unit behind the clinic. This was where the patients stayed overnight at Animal Ark, recovering from operations or perhaps for observation, until Dr. Adam or Dr. Emily had diagnosed their ailments.

Mandy yawned. The sun had sunk lower, but the evening was still warm. She could hear her father humming to himself as he fixed up the water hose and began to sprinkle the flower beds in their long, rambling garden.

"Summertime . . ." he sang, low and soulful. *"And the livin' is easy . . ."* Adam Hope put on an accent that made him sound as if he came from the American South. Mandy lay back on her lounge chair and grinned.

*"Boom-boom, b-boom . . .
So, hush, little baby,
Do-on't you-u cry-y!"*

He sprayed water over limp patches of marigolds, oom-pahing on an imaginary saxophone. Then with a grin he swung the hose around in Mandy's direction. Cold drops rained down on her striped T-shirt and hot face. She squealed and leaped to her feet.

"Da-ad!" She put her hands over her head and darted off the patio onto the grass, seeking shelter behind the apple tree.

Adam Hope, holding the hose like a fireman in an emergency, squirted water at the tree.

"Mom, help!" Mandy squealed again. She saw Emily Hope appear at the French windows, standing in her blue shorts and white sleeveless top, hands on hips, grinning at them. Mandy peered out from behind her tree. The sunlight caught in the spray, creating a million rainbow drops. "Da-ad!" Mandy yelped again. She was soaked to the skin.

Her dad pulled at the hose once too often. It stretched and jerked, then came apart at a point where a small metal clip held two sections together. Water spurted out at Adam Hope, gushing into the air and drenching him from head to foot.

"Ha!" Mandy yelled, and staggered out onto the lawn. Her sides ached from laughing. "Serves you right, Dad!" She watched water drip from his dark hair and beard. "That'll teach you to let me sunbathe in peace!"

On the patio, Dr. Emily quietly turned off the garden tap. She popped into the kitchen for two towels and came out and thrust them at her husband and Mandy. "Never trust your dad with a hose," she warned, her face bright in the sun. "He just can't resist pointing it at someone. Remember when you were little, Mandy? I'd get out the wading pool for you in the fine weather, and before I knew it, your dad would be out here in his swimming trunks, offering to 'fill it up' for me. I'd turn my back, and there he would be, squirting everyone in sight!"

Mandy laughed. Her dad sighed. "You're only young once!" he pointed out.

"Exactly!" Mandy raised her eyebrows at her mom. She'd finished toweling her hair and spread the towel over a branch to dry.

"Which reminds me of a conversation I had with Sam Western in the clinic earlier this afternoon," Dr. Adam said, growing more serious. He put his arm around his wife's shoulder and the three of them wandered back toward the house. "It had to do with enjoying yourself while you're young."

Mandy only listened with half an ear. Sam Western owned a large farm up by High Cross. He lorded it over the district and made himself unpopular with his high-handed ways, but he was a man of influence in the village. Mandy didn't care for him, because he in turn didn't care much for the animals she loved. She gathered up her tennis things as her dad chatted on about Sam Western, ready to head off to James's house.

". . . Apparently Sam Western intends to get up a petition. The town council has given permission for Bert

Burnley to set up a trailer park for the summer in his bottom field. A school from Birmingham wants to run activity camps for some of their kids. But Mr. Western tells me there's a lot of local opposition . . . Mrs. Ponsonby, Mrs. Parker Smythe, the usual crew." Dr. Adam took off his wet T-shirt and wrung it out. Then he laid it to dry across the lounge chair.

Mandy gave her mom a quick kiss and told her where she was heading.

"What can they do about it if the council has already granted planning permission?" Emily Hope twisted her long red hair onto the top of her head and glanced up at the sun. She smiled and waved at Mandy. "Don't be too late getting back," she said.

"You know Sam Western. He won't take no for an answer. If *he* objects to this scheme for the trailer park by the river, then no mere town council can stand in his way. He's planning to have a sit-in or some such nonsense when the trailers arrive. And he asked me to sign his petition against the site being used as a temporary vacation center. He says city kids will drag down the tone of the neighborhood."

Emily frowned. "You didn't sign?"

"'Course not. I said he'd best be careful to stay on the right side of the law. If the council has said yes to the vacation center, there's not much he can do about it."

"What did he say?"

"He said they'd make the council pay more attention to what residents around here think."

There was a pause as Mandy unlocked the padlock on her bike and sat on the saddle. The conversation had begun to sound interesting at the mention of kids from the city coming to stay in Welford. A summer vacation center? A trailer site by the river? This sounded like fun. There would be lots of new faces in the village, kids her own age.

"Well," Dr. Emily said, her face set in determined lines. "*I'm* a local resident, and *I* think it's a great idea!"

"Me, too," Dr. Adam agreed. "Don't worry, I don't suppose even Sam Western can put a stop to it."

"When will the trailers come on the site?"

"The day after tomorrow; Saturday, I think."

Mandy caught his last words, freewheeling down the drive toward the road. She headed between high hawthorn hedges toward the village.

The Hunters' house stood close to the river, at the far end of Welford. As she cycled easily toward James's house, Mandy passed by a level field full of buttercups and daisies. At the far side of the field there was a fence and beyond that a slope down to the riverbank. It was a couple of acres, and occasionally the farmer, Bert Burnley, would turn a herd of Friesian cows onto it. But generally the field was left fallow, a haven for rabbits and moles; undisturbed, lush, and overgrown. This was the field for the trailers, Mandy realized.

Even now there were two men climbing out of a small red pickup truck, one with a sledgehammer, one with a white sign attached to a post. The words on the sign were clear for Mandy to read as she cycled by. RIVERSIDE TRAILER PARK, it said in big black letters. The men angled the post into the ground by the edge of the field, and as Mandy pedaled the final fifty yards to James's house, she heard the thud of the hammer as it drove the post into the hard ground.

Good! she thought. It was proof that the summer camp would go ahead. I wonder whether James knows he'll have a bunch of new kids staying opposite him? She rushed inside to tell him the news.

Three

"Great!" James agreed that the trailers were a good idea. "I've always wanted to stay in one myself." He grabbed his racket and they set off for the courts.

They arrived to find James's mom already there, playing a gentle game in the early evening against Mrs. Parker Smythe from Beacon House. The Parker Smythes were rich neighbors of Sam Western, and Mandy wasn't surprised to hear the topic of conversation as the two ladies finished their game and came off court to rest.

"I mean to say!" Mrs. Parker Smythe's voice rang out above the smack of tennis rackets against balls on nearby courts. She was cool and elegant in her short white skirt, not a blond hair out of place. Mandy easily heard every word she said. "Who knows what sort of people we'll have coming to stay in the village? And trailers are such a glaring eyesore. Why, we might even be able to see them from our house! And these children will all come from the cities, and you can guess what they'll do once they're let loose on a quiet little village like Welford. Your house faces right onto the field, doesn't it?" she asked James's mom. "You must be seething with anger!"

Mandy frowned as she trotted to the net to retrieve two balls. Mrs. Parker Smythe was being her usual snobbish self.

"Well, actually, no, we're not," Mrs. Hunter said more quietly. "We weren't keen on the idea of trailers when we first heard, it's true. But then we realized it would be just for the summer, and we thought what a lovely opportunity it was. Not just for the children who will come here on vacation, but for James and all the village children, too. It's time they broadened their horizons, don't you think?" She looked Mrs. Parker Smythe full in the face without toning down her opinion. As she turned away to go up the steps into the pavilion, she gave James and Mandy a small wink.

"Well!" Mrs. Parker Smythe stood there stranded. She swiped at the grass with her tennis racket and looked daggers at Mandy. "There are plenty of people around here who take the opposite view!" she announced to nobody in particular, as she flounced up the steps after Mrs. Hunter.

Mandy and James played fast and furious tennis, in spite of the heat. They called it a draw at one set each, promising to take up the challenge again next time. They flopped down by the net to take a swig of orange juice that Mandy had brought along in her bag.

"How about an ice cream?" James suggested.

Mandy nodded and they were soon on their bikes cycling back toward the village, past the newly erected sign.

"I'm glad your mom put Mrs. Parker Smythe in her place," Mandy said, glancing at the empty field. But she knew that Mr. Western and Mrs. Parker Smythe were not the sort to give in easily. She wasn't surprised to see a small knot of people gathered together up ahead, standing around the low silver car belonging to Mrs. Parker Smythe that was parked just outside the post office in the center of the village. She could hear arguments flying back and forth. Feelings were running high.

"I think it's an absolute disgrace!" Mrs. Ponsonby proclaimed. Her Pekingese dog, Pandora, sat growling at her feet. "The whole village will be swamped by strangers, and these city children aren't brought up to follow the country code! They'll leave gates open and sheep will wander onto the roads. They won't keep to public footpaths as they should, and they will climb walls, you mark my words!" Somehow, the fusspot of Welford managed to make it sound like a hanging offense. "And goodness knows what else they'll do!" she said darkly.

Mandy got off her bike and passed by the group, pausing to stroke Pandora and Mrs. Ponsonby's lovable mongrel, Toby. Ernie Bell sat on the bench outside the post office, listening quietly. He shook his head. "I reckon we should hold our horses before we all go overboard," he warned. "We mustn't give a dog a bad name, you know."

A strange, muddled picture of horses, ships, and dogs jumbled in Mandy's mind, but she agreed with Ernie; the visitors should be given a fair chance.

She followed James into the cool, shaded interior of the McFarlanes' shop to buy their ice cream. When they came out, Mrs. Parker Smythe was still gathering support for the antitrailer campaign. "Our first aim must be to stop them moving onto the site in the first place," she ordered. "It's all very well for Mr. Burnley to wave his planning permission all over the place, but he's flying in the face of important local opinion."

Mrs. Ponsonby no[...], trotted up t[...] out, gazing longingly [...]

"The first trailers a[...]ing," Mrs. Parker Smy[...] their way in the road[...] to drive tractors dow[...] the field. We must all[...]

Ernie cleared his t[...]oat. the police station in Walton?" he said to the small crowd. "It's against the law to obstruct a public highway, remember!"

Mandy and James agreed. She was concentrating so hard on the argument that her ice cream cone tipped sideways, and the half-melted contents slipped out. But it had no chance to hit the ground; Toby caught it like a soccer player diving for a catch in the goal. He gobbled it in one gulp. Mandy's mouth dropped open in surprise.

"Shh!" James warned. If Mrs. Ponsonby found out she'd be rushing poor Toby straight over to Animal Ark with a near-fatal case of *frozen stomachitis*! Meanwhile, Pandora shuffled across to stare up at James's ice cream.

"We must be prepared to stand by our principles!" Mrs. Ponsonby took up the argument against the new trailers. "We must make it clear that Welford is against

rt, made without a by-your-leave." She
double chin and pulled back her shoul-
oldier on parade. The frills down the front
wder-blue dress shook with outrage.

s slipped Pandora the remains of his ice cream,
e and all. He'd been won over by the Pekingese's
uge, dark eyes. The ice cream disappeared in a flash.

"Toby, Pandora, come here!" Mrs. Ponsonby clapped her plump hands for their attention. "Come here, good doggies!"

They both yawned and ignored her.

"Go on, Pandora. Go on, Toby!" Mandy whispered.

Reluctantly they obeyed her and trotted toward their owner.

Mrs. Parker Smythe had started up the smooth engine of her silver car, and Mrs. Ponsonby began to make her way up the street, head held high. People began to disperse, grumbling and muttering about the new trailer site.

Mandy looked at Ernie scratching his stubbly gray head. He gazed back at James and Mandy. "Some folks around here don't have enough to do to keep them out of mischief," he complained. "And you know what they say; the devil makes work for idle hands."

Soon the street was empty. As the sun began to sink, a golden red glow seeped into the sky. Mandy said good-bye to James, ready to head for home. "Let's keep our fingers crossed," she said, her mind flying back for a moment to the really important and interesting things in life: animals, and more specifically, their hopes of looking after Henry.

"We'll find out tomorrow morning," he reminded her.

"Let's get to school ten minutes early," she suggested. "To see if Miss Temple's picked out the name."

They arranged to meet outside the post office at eight o'clock, then they rode off on their separate ways. James waved at Ernie and passed by the new sign for the trailer site. Then he turned right, up his driveway. Mandy rode up her street toward the sunset, taking James's advice and thinking positive thoughts. "We *will* be lucky," she said over and over. "We *will* be lucky and get to look after Henry for the summer!"

They gathered outside the biology lab before morning homeroom; Mandy and James, Vicki Simpson and her friend Becky Severn, and Brandon Gill, who lived at Graystones Farm. Altogether, Mandy counted twenty-three hopefuls, all waiting to see who would look after the school hamster.

She peered through the window into the empty lab. In one corner she spotted Henry's cage, a roomy, hardwood box with a removable glass front and a wire-mesh lid. Inside the box was a day area covered in fresh hay, with a drinking bowl in one corner. And there was a small "upstairs" compartment, a box within a box, that Henry could enter via a ramp. He used this private bedroom for his frequent daytime naps. And of course, in one corner was the exercise wheel.

Mandy could see him now, trundling away. He reminded her of a stout man jogging for his health, determined to get his daily exercise. She nudged James and pointed to the cage. "Look at him." She smiled.

"It will do him good," he assured her. "Did you know, they found out that some hamsters run five miles a night on those exercise wheels?"

Mandy let this sink in. "Five miles? Then why is he so fat?"

"I didn't say that *Henry* runs five miles," James pointed out. "He probably just comes out to use the wheel when he knows someone's looking, to show off. I bet Henry just snacks and snoozes the night away!"

"Are you saying he's lazy?" Mandy pretended she wouldn't hear a word said against the hamster. "If you ask me, it's not his fault he's fat."

"Whose is it, then?"

"It's all those people who feed him chips from their lunch boxes, obviously! You can't blame a poor little hamster for eating all the wrong, fattening foods, can you?"

"Hmm." James looked thoughtful. "I suppose not."

Mandy nodded and looked up the corridor. "Hurry up, Miss Temple!" she pleaded. She noticed Vicki Simpson whispering behind her hand to Becky. She ignored this and smiled at Brandon. "How's Ruby?" she asked. Ruby was Brandon's pet pig.

"Great," Brandon said in his broad, no-nonsense way. "We're going over to Walton this weekend to show her. We think we have a chance to win a prize."

Mandy was wishing him luck when Miss Temple appeared at the end of the corridor. She walked briskly toward them. Everyone fell silent. All eyes were on the young teacher as she unlocked the lab and invited them in.

"Sit down for a moment." She put down her bag and turned toward them. "Now, I haven't drawn the name yet. I wanted you all to see that it's fair and aboveboard." She picked up a cardboard box. "Since I haven't got a hat, this will have to do. All the names are in here on folded pieces of paper."

Mandy fixed her eyes on the box. We *will* be lucky! she repeated silently to herself.

Miss Temple smiled at them all. "We only have a few moments before the bell rings for homeroom," she said. "So who wants to pick the name out of the box?"

A forest of hands shot up.

"Becky, you're nearest. You come and do it for us." Miss Temple held the box up above eye level so Becky couldn't see which paper she chose. "Just reach up and draw one out. That's it."

Becky stood on tiptoe. Mandy held her breath and kept her fingers crossed. She watched as Becky took a piece of paper from the box and handed it to Miss Temple. The teacher unfolded it and laid it flat on the bench.

She looked along the rows. "James Hunter," she announced, clear as a bell.

James gasped. Mandy couldn't believe her ears. Several of the others smiled wistfully and shuffled off. Miss Temple held open the door and said sorry to the unlucky ones. But Becky frowned and muttered to Vicki, ". . . Seems a bit suspicious to me . . . can't be coincidence . . . Mandy is teacher's pet, we all know that . . . James Hunter is her best friend!"

Vicki nodded. "It was probably all a big fix."

Miss Temple, busy now telling James where to find her after school, overheard them. She turned to speak. "Vicki, Becky, I'm sorry you're disappointed," she said quietly. "But so are about twenty other people. I can't let you go around school all day with those long faces. You just have to accept the luck of the draw." She waited patiently until the two girls returned her gaze. "That's better. And don't let me hear that you've been spreading false rumors that this was all done out of favoritism. It was nothing of the kind, as you very well know."

Vicki and Becky blushed. "Yes, Miss Temple. Sorry, Miss Temple," they said.

"Well, go off to homeroom, and we'll hear no more about a fix. You, too, Mandy and James, or else you'll all be in trouble for being late."

They nodded and hurried down the corridor, hard on the heels of the two disgruntled girls. Only now could Mandy begin to believe their luck. She gave a little skip and a jump.

"What did I tell you about the power of positive thinking?" James grinned. They took the stairs two at a time.

"Pure luck!" Mandy teased.

"Says you!" Before he split off down a separate corridor, he paused. "You know Henry's weight problem?" he reminded her.

She caught his eye. "Can I guess what you're thinking?"

"I'm thinking fresh vegetables, dried oats, nuts, and bread!"

"No more chips?" She began to smile. "James, you're planning to put Henry on a diet!"

"A calorie count," he confirmed.

"A strict diet."

"An exercise plan, so we can bring him back in September looking like a new hamster. No more excess fat." He grinned.

"Poor Henry." Mandy shook her head. "I suppose it's for his own good, though."

"Poor Henry, nothing! My house is going to be the first hamster health farm in the country. What do you think, Mandy?"

She pondered the challenge. "You're right," she decided. "No cookies, no cakes!"

"Good. See you at four in the lab?" he asked. They would take Henry home together.

"You bet!" She sped off to her own classroom. They had Henry to themselves for the whole summer. They'd give him the best of everything and make him stick to his healthy diet. They might even be able to take him on outings, down to the river for a picnic in the fresh air. Mandy made great plans. She sat at her desk just as her homeroom teacher, Mr. Meldrum, arrived. Her head was in the clouds, doting on Henry, when he called her name from the register.

"Mandy Hope?" he repeated sharply.

"Yes, Mr. Meldrum!" she called. Four o'clock couldn't come soon enough. Then the whole summer vacation was spread before them, endless days of looking after Henry!

Four

It was early Saturday morning. Mandy had been up for ages, busy doing chores at Animal Ark before Simon, their nurse, had even arrived. She cleaned out cages and talked to the parrot, the gerbil, and the black Labrador who'd been kept overnight in the unit. She knew that good hygiene was a top priority for a vet, and anyway, she loved the company of animals, talking to them and encouraging them to get back on their feet after an illness.

Simon came in promptly at half past eight to find everyone spotless and ready for office hours. He chatted with Mandy for a few minutes while Jean Knox, the receptionist, prepared the appointment list. "What's it feel like to have six whole weeks of freedom?" he asked.

"Great!" Mandy bubbled with enthusiasm. She took off her white coat and hung it on a peg in one of the treatment rooms. "James has brought home the school hamster for the summer. We're going to take him down to the river for a picnic."

"Lucky hamster," Simon said with a grin. He was young and easygoing. "I had a hamster when I was a kid. She was called Honey; a light golden one with beautiful ruby eyes. But she couldn't see a foot in front of her nose. Hamsters can't, you know. They're very nearsighted."

Mandy nodded and made a mental note.

"They use their whiskers to feel their way around. They're nocturnal, sleepy by day and active by night."

Again Mandy nodded. "Henry won't come to any harm if we take him on outings, will he?"

Simon smiled. "He'll think he's in seventh heaven. I take it he's tame?"

"Very. He likes to be out of his cage. He sits in your hand and loves being stroked. And fed! That's his problem, actually."

Simon smiled. "Just watch what you give him to eat, that's all. No chocolate for a start. It's poisonous for hamsters. Apples are fine. Sunflower seeds are their favorite, and full of protein. They love cookies and cake as well, but not too often."

Mandy's face lit up. "We plan to put him on a diet; fruit and greens, nuts and cereals. No sugar. We want him to lose weight."

"Very good." Simon followed her into reception and smiled at Jean, fixing his glasses firmly on his nose. "Does Henry know about this diet plan?"

"Not yet." Mandy had reached the door, eager to be on her way down to James's house.

"Best of luck," he called. "And remember, be strict with Henry. Don't let him get around you with those big, soft eyes. I know you!" He laughed as he watched her swing her leg over her bicycle saddle.

"Could you tell Mom I won't be back for lunch?" Mandy called before she sped off. "Mrs. Hunter's making us a picnic lunch and we're taking Henry out for his treat!" She whizzed down the lane. The sun was still shining, the trees rustled in a slight breeze; a perfect day for a picnic.

Mandy lay flat on her back. The nearby river rippled and swirled, the sand was warm in the sun.

"Pass me another lettuce leaf for Henry," James murmured. He sat cross-legged on the pebbles, with the hamster nestled in the palm of his hand. Henry was lazily grooming behind his ears with his tiny front paws. His cage was set carefully to one side.

Mandy reached out an arm and felt for the picnic basket that James's mom had packed. Her fingers made contact with the wickerwork top. She flipped it open and rummaged inside without raising her head to look. Sun, sandwiches, and lemonade had made her sleepy.

James got up, balancing Henry in his hand. "Don't worry, I'll do it. Anyway, why are you in such a lazy mood?"

"I'll have you know I was up at the crack of dawn!" She sighed. She opened one eye as James crouched beside the basket. Henry's nose and whiskers twitched with interest.

"James, watch out!" Mandy sat bolt upright, but her cry came too late. Henry had launched himself from the palm of James's hand, straight into the basket. He landed with a thud among the leftover cookies. Real food! Beautiful calories! He started eating happily.

James panicked. He hadn't seen where Henry had landed. "Where is he? Quick, Mandy, where's he gone?" He scrambled a few yards up the bank into some long grass. "Henry's escaped. Help me look!"

Mandy gazed down at a happy hamster. "He's in here," she said calmly. "In the basket." She knelt for a closer look. "Oh, Henry!" she scolded. She heard James creep up behind her. Together they peered into the shadowy safety of the picnic basket. Henry was nibbling cookies to his heart's content. He munched and stored the crumbs in his cheeks, shoving them into his mouth as fast as he could. Mandy glanced at James.

"Henry, the calories!" James shook his head.

"A lot he cares!" Mandy began to smile. "And it's no good offering him lettuce now, not when there's a heap of broken cookies to get at!"

Henry cocked his head at them. His bright eyes twinkled, his cheeks pouched out to twice their normal size.

"Come here, Henry." James reached into the basket and cupped both hands under Henry's fat little belly. He tried to sound severe, but a grin was spreading over his face, too. "So much for getting you slim! Oh, well, it could have been worse."

"How come?"

"He could have actually made a run for it, I suppose. It would have taken us all afternoon to find him in that long grass. Thank heavens he landed in the picnic basket."

Mandy shook her head. "Henry knows which side his bread is buttered on," she said. Then she giggled.

"Or which way the cookie crumbles!" James laughed. "But it's ruined his diet. We'll have to make him have an extra run on his wheel tonight, and nothing but lettuce for him tomorrow!"

Henry twitched his nose.

"I don't think he likes that idea." Mandy watched James carry the hamster back to his cage. "Time to be getting back," she said. She tidied the basket and closed its lid. "I promised Dad I'd lend a hand with afternoon office hours."

Henry's little escapade had brought them back to earth. It was all very well drifting through the sunny day on the riverbank like this, but there were jobs to do. She sighed as she stood up and straightened her T-shirt. "Hey," she said, glancing beyond the river into the field beyond. "What's going on over there?"

There was a cluster of cars gathering on the narrow road. Two tractors came trundling down the lane after them, and a group of people stood by the gate into the field, talking loudly.

"It's that group protesting about the trailers," James said. He picked up the hamster cage and climbed onto the path. "Mrs. Ponsonby and the rest."

Mandy spied a wide-brimmed pink hat in the middle of the small crowd. And then she recognized Mrs. Parker Smythe's low silver car. In the distance, she saw a huge truck pulling the first of the trailers. It crawled slowly toward the recently formed roadblock. Voices rose. Someone brought out a sign and raised it in the air.

"Come on!" Mandy said, picking up the basket. "Let's cut across and see what's going on!"

By the time they reached the gate, the protest was well under way. A second truck with its enormous load had pulled up behind the first. James spotted a police car bringing up the rear and pointed it out to Mandy. "Police escort," he whispered. "This could be serious!"

But Mandy couldn't help smiling at the gang of activists. They were an odd bunch to be breaking the law. Mrs. Parker Smythe, more at home at a cocktail party, tried to look the part of a protester in a pair of well-cut black trousers and a crisp white shirt. But Mrs. Ponsonby looked as if she was dressed for a garden party, in her flower-laden hat and tight-fitting dress. Her stout face was red with the effort of protest, as she waved her cardboard sign high in the air. NO WELCOME TO TRAILERS IN WELFORD! it said on one side, WELFORD SAYS NO TO THE TRAILERS! on the other.

The two women took their orders, along with five or six other protesters, from the sturdy figure of Mr. Western, who stood and directed operations like an army major. "Watch your right flank!" he warned as Bert Burnley, the farmer who'd agreed to have the trailers on his land, came down the hill from his farm.

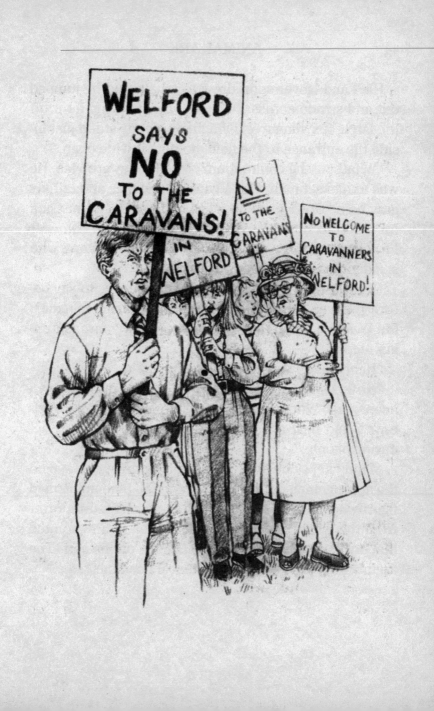

His Land Rover soon drew to a halt, and he jumped out and strode across. He seized the gate and let it off the latch. It swung free. Obligingly Mandy stood just inside the entrance to the field, holding it wide open.

"What's all the commotion?" Mr. Burnley growled. He was a thickset man with a wide, ruddy face and crinkly gray hair. "Don't you know I've had council permission for this since Easter? Why not pack up and go home, or I'll get the police to act!" He glared at Sam Western, who strode toward him, hands on hips.

"Why don't you listen to what people have to say before you rush ahead with your money-grabbing scheme?" Mr. Western shouted, inches from the burly farmer's angry face.

"Hear, hear!" Mrs. Ponsonby chimed in.

"Now, hang on just a minute." Mr. Burnley's frown deepened. "Who are you calling money-grabbing, Western? You'd best check your facts before you start accusing people!"

Mandy kept one eye on the arguing men, one eye on the approaching policeman. Behind the blue-uniformed figure she caught sight of a young, fair-haired reporter from the local paper, camera at the ready. She pointed him out to James. "The newspaper's in on the act!" The argument could develop into a local headline.

Mr. Western snorted. His supporters rallied around as the policeman, the reporter, and two drivers skirted around Western's tractors that were blocking the road.

"I said, check your facts," Burnley roared. "And you'll find I'm letting the trailers use this field rent-free. It's for a good cause, and I've told Kingsmill School to go ahead and give the kids a proper vacation, free of charge. It's time someone around here did something for nothing!" He squared up to Mr. Western, red in the face. Mrs. Ponsonby, Mrs. Parker Smythe, and the others looked taken aback.

"Hear, hear!" Mandy and James cried.

Mr. Western blustered. "Well, whether or not you're lining your own pockets, Bert Burnley, we still don't want the eyesore of a whole lot of trailers spoiling the look of the place. And we won't budge from here until you tell those truck drivers to back off down that lane and take those trailers back where they came from!"

He didn't see the tall figure of the policeman loom up behind him, but Mandy and James did. They saw the reporter raise his camera and start to take shots of the protesters and their signs. They heard them fall quiet in the full glare of publicity. One or two crept away to their cars before they could be photographed.

"This will be in the paper on Monday," someone whispered. "I never bargained for that." He went and sat quietly in his car, looking as if he wished the ground would swallow him.

But Mrs. Ponsonby stood firm. She glared at the young policeman as he approached Sam Western and ordered him to tell his men to move their tractors. "Welford Says No!" she chanted.

The journalist wrote notes: Mr. Western argued their case.

It was all to no avail. The policeman sternly pointed out that what they were doing was against the law. Mandy and James stood alongside Mr. Burnley, happy to be photographed. "We think it's a great idea," Mandy told the reporter. "Everyone should be able to come and enjoy the countryside. We're looking forward to meeting these new kids. And I'd just like to say that not many people in Welford are against the idea of the trailer park. I think you should put that in your article!"

Mrs. Parker Smythe overheard and tossed her head. Mrs. Ponsonby glowered. But Mandy and James stood, one to either side of Mr. Burnley, proudly facing the camera, under the bright new sign for Riverside Trailer Park.

"Thanks. It should make the front page on Monday," the reporter told them.

"By the way, did you get Henry in the photograph?"

Mandy asked. They watched as the policeman cleared off the protesters. Gradually the sit-in fell apart. Mrs. Ponsonby stopped chanting and lowered her sign. Mr. Western at last gave an order for the tractors to back off.

"Who's Henry?" The journalist packed away his notebook and camera, ready to dash off to file his report.

"The hamster." Mandy pointed to the cage, where Henry stared contentedly at the proceedings, his cheeks still pleasantly full of cookies.

"Oh, yes; the hamster's in the shot, don't you worry," the reporter said with a smile.

And so the protest faded. The protesters went home, red-faced and grumbling, unused to losing an argument. Then the trucks trundled onto the field with their huge trailers, while Mr. Burnley shook hands with a young man and woman; two teachers from Kingsmill School who were organizing the vacation center.

"Thanks very much," the young man said to Mandy, when he heard from the farmer the part Mandy and James had played.

Mandy blushed. "We were glad to help."

She and James said hello to the young woman, Chrissie Searle. The man was called Pete Cavendish. Both leaders were young and pleasant-looking outdoor types in shorts and T-shirts. But they were too busy to stop and talk for long. "The first batch of kids is due to arrive on Monday," Pete Cavendish said. "And there's loads to do before then."

Satisfied, they went their separate ways. Full of the latest news, James and Mandy went back to his house with Henry. Then Mandy hurried on home, past the wooden sign with ANIMAL ARK, VETERINARY CLINIC carved on it, and into the house to tell her mom and dad she'd be in the newspaper. The protest had collapsed, the trailers were moving in, and Mr. Western had admitted defeat.

Emily Hope smiled and gave her a hug. "That's my girl!" she said after she'd listened to what Mandy had said to the reporter. "I couldn't have put it better myself!"

Five

There was no doubt about it, Sam Western and his followers had made fools of themselves. Everyone at Animal Ark agreed that their picture on the front page of the newspaper on Monday morning made them out to be small-minded snobs. Mandy's own quote made the headline: "A GREAT IDEA!" she read in bold black capitals. Underneath the one of the protesters there was another good, clear picture of James holding Henry's cage, standing alongside Mr. Burnley and Mandy, with a caption that read, "Supporters of the trailer site."

Mandy beamed across the breakfast table at her grandma and grandpa. They'd dropped in to show her the newspaper on their way back home from the village. Lilac Cottage, their pretty house, was down the road from Animal Ark.

"So when do we expect the first arrivals?" Grandpa asked.

"This morning. Pete and Chrissie have had to work like mad to get things ready. There are six trailers on the site, and a big Winnebago in the middle of the field, for a shop and a clubhouse combined. They've got things really well organized now."

"Pete and Chrissie?" Grandma interrupted.

"Pete Cavendish and Chrissie Searle. They're the teachers from Kingsmill School in Birmingham."

"And you're on first-name terms already?" Grandma teased.

"Yes. I think they're great. They plan to take the kids canoeing and mountain biking for a start, and if the weather stays fine, there's going to be a barbecue by the river at the end of the week!" Mandy was up on her feet, gulping down the last of her orange juice. "Sorry, Grandma, sorry, Grandpa; I have to run. I promised James I'd meet him in the village. We want to go and say hello to the first group when they arrive. Chrissie said she thought it would help to make them feel more at home. They're bound to find things pretty strange here in Welford if they come from a big city like Birmingham!"

She gave her grandparents a quick kiss and was on her way, grabbing her bike and whizzing down the lane.

James, ready and waiting in the yard outside the Fox and Goose, waved a greeting. "I saw the Kingsmill minibus turn down our road five minutes ago," he told her. They pedaled together down the main street.

Mandy nodded. "How's Henry?"

"Great. He's back on his diet again — sunflower seeds and slices of apple. I left his cage in the fresh air on the front porch. Mom says she'll keep an eye on him."

They cycled easily and quickly along the flat stretch of road. Up ahead, over the tops of the hawthorn hedges, they could see the gleaming new trailers in Mr. Burnley's field.

"Okay?" Mandy asked. They propped their bikes against the gate and went into the field.

She felt suddenly shy as she stepped through the long grass toward the gray Winnebago. But she thought how much more strange things must seem to the newcomers who sat on the grass outside the hut, looking warily at her and James as they approached.

"Hi," she said to a sea of faces; a dozen or so kids of

about her own age, some propped back on their elbows, some lounging against the wall of the hut, some pretending not to notice her and James. Mandy saw one girl standing apart from the rest. She was small and skinny, with wild red hair and gray-green eyes. "I'm Mandy Hope," she said. "I live here in Welford."

The girl stared shyly back. She nodded but didn't open her mouth to speak.

"Never mind her," one boy said. "You can't get a word out of her. Anyone for a game of soccer?" He picked up a white plastic ball and rolled it into the space in front of the hut.

Several voices chorused yes. James nodded, glad to join in. Soon the ball was being kicked up and down the field to the sound of excited yells, calls of fouls, and claims for penalty kicks.

Mandy grinned at the shy girl. "Who's the boy with the ball?" she asked. He dribbled the ball expertly and passed it, shouting out instructions.

"Paul." The answer came out almost a whisper.

"And who's the girl with the blond hair?"

"Sonia."

Mandy tried her best to commit their names to memory. "Who are you?"

"Leanne Jackson." The girl delivered her own name

with a blush that colored her whole face. "I'm new at Kingsmill."

"Are you all from the same school?"

"Yes, but I've only been there since May. My mom and I had to move. That's why I changed schools again."

Mandy went carefully ahead. She glanced at Leanne, then back at the soccer game. "My mom's got the same color hair as you. Only, she's not my actual mom. My real mom and dad died in an accident just after I was born. I'm adopted."

Leanne raised her eyes from the buttercups at her feet and stared at Mandy. "Have you got a dad?"

Mandy nodded. "He's the local vet. So's my mom. He's lived in Welford all his life."

A sigh escaped from Leanne. "A vet? Have you got loads and loads of animals at your house?"

"Sort of. Only, they're not mine; they're patients at the clinic. Dogs, cats, rabbits, donkeys, ponies, you name it. Oh, and I do have three pet rabbits of my own."

Leanne sighed again. "Lucky thing."

"Don't you have any pets?" Mandy was happy to chat on about her favorite subject. The two of them sat down cross-legged on the grass, one eye on the noisy game. Sonia, in goal, saved one of Paul's shots. A fresh cheer went up.

"No, I'm not allowed," Leanne said. "My mom and I live in an apartment, and we can't keep pets."

Mandy said she thought it was a shame. Behind her shyness, Leanne seemed friendly and easy to talk to.

"I'd love to have one," she went on wistfully. "A pet all my own to look after, I mean. I've always wanted to. But we move around too much. My mom says it wouldn't be fair to an animal."

"I suppose so." Mandy thought for a second. "Listen, Leanne, why don't we go over to James's house? I'm sure he won't mind, and there's something I'd like to show you. He lives just across the road; it won't take long!"

Slowly, awkwardly, Leanne got to her feet. "Okay."

"Great!" Mandy led the way out of the field, across the narrow road. They jogged past Claire MacKay's house, where the sign ROSA'S REFUGE hung from a tree in the yard. "Claire looks after hedgehogs," Mandy explained. "She's quite new to the village, but she soon settled in once she'd set up the refuge." She smiled at Leanne as they went through James's gate and up the path.

James's Labrador must have heard their footsteps, for he came bounding down the side of the house, tail wagging. Mandy gave him a hug. "This is Blackie," she said to Leanne. "And the little cat asleep on the mat is Eric."

Leanne went up the step and bent to stroke his soft, warm head. Eric purred. "He's lovely," she sighed.

Mandy pointed to the wooden cage on a shelf on the front porch. "And this is Henry."

"A hamster!" Leanne's eyes lit up. "Oh, he's gorgeous!"

Henry, aware of his admiring audience, responded by jumping into the exercise wheel. He set it in motion with his feet, easily keeping his balance as he scurried forward.

"He's a golden hamster. He's six months old. He belongs to our school, but James is looking after him for the summer," Mandy explained, glad to see Leanne's face beaming down at Henry. "Do you know much about hamsters? They're desert rodents. They're hoarders." She reeled off the facts.

"I know. Born in a litter of six to ten infants, without hair. Eyes open on the twelfth day. Life span two to three years."

"Hey!" Mandy was impressed.

"I've read all about them in my pets book. But I've never actually been this close to one before." She gazed into the cage as Henry clambered out of the wheel and came up to the front of the cage, whiskers twitching.

"Would you like to hold him?"

Leanne nodded. She held her breath as Mandy

cupped her hands under Henry, lifted him out of the cage, and gave him to her. Henry nibbled her finger, then nestled contentedly in her palm. "Oh!" she said, speechless.

"I expect you'll be able to come and see Henry whenever you like," Mandy promised. "James won't mind. And I come down here most days, to help look after him. Staying at Riverside means you're really close at hand."

With her free hand Leanne stroked Henry's golden coat. "He's so soft! His feet tickle!"

"Try giving him this." Mandy handed her a slice of apple from a plastic bag on the shelf. She watched as the hamster took it and began to nibble. They both smiled.

At last, Leanne reached forward to put Henry back in his cage. "I'd better be going." The smile had begun to fade.

"But you'll come again?"

"Yes, please."

Mandy fastened the lock. Leanne took a last look at Henry, then stroked Eric as Mandy went to play in the yard with Blackie. Just then, Mrs. Hunter stuck her head through the kitchen window and waved. "Hello, Mandy!"

"Hi, Mrs. Hunter. This is Leanne Jackson from Birmingham."

"Hello, Leanne. Nice to meet you. I hope you have a good time here in Welford." Mrs. Hunter smiled and turned back to Mandy. "Can you tell James to come home for lunch at twelve-thirty?"

Mandy promised; then she and her new friend headed back for the trailer field. By the time they got there, the soccer game was coming to an end, with a three–two victory for Paul's team. Leanne nodded quietly at Mandy and slipped away to her trailer before the crowd of thirsty players charged up to the camp store for cans of Coke.

James, already part of the gang, introduced Mandy to Ben, a tall boy with bristly hair. Ben was a joker and obviously crazy about clothes. He wore all the latest sports gear, pleased to have the others looking up to him. Mandy smiled and settled in with the crowd, soon forgetting about lonely Leanne.

"What shall we do now?" Sonia demanded with a yawn. She came out of the store and flopped to the ground. "Not much going on around here, is there?"

Her friend Marcie sprinkled a handful of daisy petals in her hair. "Stop moaning, Sonia." Marcie's broad face was cheerful and friendly. She grinned up at Mandy. "She never stops complaining, that's her problem."

"Yes, I do. The country's boring, that's all!" Sonia

stared at the hillside. "Nothing happens. No stores, no coffee bars. I don't know why I said I'd come!"

"See!" Marcie laughed.

"Aagh, what was that?" Sonia squirmed and tried to wriggle one arm up the back of her T-shirt. "Something's alive in there! Ouch! Get it out, Marcie!" She sprang up, yelping and dancing around in panic.

"Stand still!" Marcie giggled. She fished about and pulled a flattened daisy from under her friend's shirt. "Very alive, I'm sure!"

Sonia scowled and flounced off to her trailer. "Well! Anyway, I hate the countryside!" she wailed.

Mandy turned to Ben, who was trying to persuade a red-eyed boy called Sean to go swimming in the river. "James says it's not that deep. And I bet it's warm! Come on, what are we waiting for?"

"I dunno." Sean frowned. "I think I'm allergic to something around here." His light brown hair flopped over his forehead, his brown eyes streamed.

"Hay fever?" Mandy suggested.

Sean groaned. "Call this a vacation? Just stick me down on a beach somewhere hot like Spain or Greece, will you? I can't stand all these flowers!"

"There's a beach by the river," James suggested. "And if you stay by the water, your hay fever won't be so bad." He ran ahead, followed by Ben and a reluctant Sean.

Mandy watched the field empty as all the Kingsmill kids went off in different directions. They were a mixed bunch, and they hadn't all settled in yet, but she'd taken to Leanne from the start. She hoped to see her again soon. Waving at Chrissie Searle inside the store, Mandy went to get her bike and rode slowly back to Animal Ark.

By early Wednesday morning, Mandy found that the freedom to come and go as she pleased had really sunk in. She loved the feeling of not being tied to school routine. It meant she was able to help out more at the clinic, and to ride her bike around the village, or to visit friends up on farms.

But there was already gossip in the village about the children at Riverside. There was talk in McFarlanes' when Mandy popped in for postage stamps for her grandma. Mrs. Ponsonby was in the thick of it, of course, advising Susan Price not to get mixed up with the newcomers. "They're a thoroughly bad lot," she warned. "I'm sure your parents wouldn't want you to mix with them, Susan dear."

Susan was in her riding gear. She made a secret grimace at Mandy. "Thanks, Mrs. Ponsonby," she said breezily. "Anyway, I'm riding Prince in the competition over at Kenley next week, so I've got a lot of work on my hands to get him up to scratch."

"Quite right; keep you out of mischief." As the shop bell rang and Susan made her escape down the steps, Mrs. Ponsonby turned to Mr. McFarlane to report the latest wrongdoings of the city children. "They've been here less than three days, and already they've caused havoc in the village! They have left gates open, of course, and it had to be on poor Mr. Western's land, just as I said, and Dennis Saville had to round up several cows from the field road. It's a wonder none of the poor beasts was injured!"

"Are they sure it was the children from Riverside, Mrs. Ponsonby?" Mr. McFarlane slowly weighed out a half pound of mint toffees.

"Of course. Mr. Western saw them with his own eyes. And the noise from the site is dreadful. Loud music until late at night. Wild games. Shrieking and shouting and playing in the river. I wouldn't be surprised if someone drowned!" Mrs. Ponsonby took off her pink-framed glasses and wiped them on a tiny lace handkerchief. She fixed them primly back on her nose, then turned to Mandy. "You can't say I didn't warn you!" she said in triumph.

Mandy bit her tongue. "Five first-class stamps, please," she said to the shopkeeper as Mrs. Ponsonby took her bag of candy and sailed out of the shop.

She must have been scowling because Mr. McFarlane winked and said, "Don't mind her."

"That's all very well, but other people might believe what she says," Mandy grumbled. She didn't want Mrs. Ponsonby to spoil things for the Riverside crowd. So far they had enjoyed their mountain biking and canoeing activities, and there had been no major incidents, but Mrs. Ponsonby and Mrs. Parker Smythe kept their eagle eyes constantly open, and Mr. Western was poised to send off his petition to the council at the first sign of real trouble. Mandy paid for the stamps and made her way out with a shake of her head.

But she was stopped in her tracks by a scene in the heart of the village. A group, including Ernie Bell and his friend Walter Pickard, with Betty Hilder from the animal sanctuary and Mandy's friend John Hardy from the pub, had gathered by Walter's garden wall. In their midst, Mrs. Ponsonby stood examining fresh evidence.

"You say they were standing on your wall?" she asked in a loud voice.

They stared at something lying at their feet. With a sinking heart, Mandy got off her bike and went to take a look.

"Same as always," Walter agreed. "It's a nice sunny position, see."

Peering over the wall, among the feet of the bystanders, Mandy could see the remains of clay flowerpots, scattered earth, and half a dozen uprooted geranium plants. They were all trampled into the flagstones in Walter's yard. She glanced up at the old man's dismayed face. She knew he tended his plants with care. The geraniums brightened up the row of little stone cottages year after year, and Walter could hardly afford to replace them at this time. Whoever had done this must have been acting out of mischief, not knowing how much the flowers meant to him.

"Did you see who did it?" Ernie asked, his voice tense with annoyance.

Walter shook his head. "I just opened the door to collect my milk from the step and there they were, all smashed!"

"It's obvious," Mrs. Ponsonby told them. "Didn't I tell you that those children from the trailer site were running wild? I knew there'd be some serious damage before too long!" She fixed them with her beady eyes.

"But you can't be sure," Betty Hilder objected. "Not if Walter didn't actually see them do it."

"It stands to reason. We never had a moment's trouble in the village before those young hooligans came along. Now every day there's something new. Cattle on the loose. Loud late-night parties. And now vandalism!" Mrs. Ponsonby let this last word roll richly around her tongue.

"Hmm." Walter shook his head. "Whoever it is, it won't stick them pots back together, and it won't revive them poor geraniums, neither."

"But I did try to warn you all," Mrs. Ponsonby insisted. "I knew that the trailer site spelled trouble, only none of you would listen." She sniffed and glared at

Mandy. "Well, I hope you're satisfied!" she said, stalking off down the street.

Shaken, Mandy couldn't find the nerve to defend the city children in front of poor Walter. Betty ran to the pub for a broom to begin clearing up the mess, while Ernie took his friend to his own cottage for a cup of tea.

It's only a few flowers, Mandy told herself, and nobody even knew for sure whether they'd been knocked over by accident or on purpose. But she knew it looked bad. The campaign to get the trailers out would latch onto just this kind of mystery.

"Do you really think it was them?" John Hardy whispered to Mandy. His studious face waited earnestly for an answer.

"No, I don't," she said slowly. "But try telling that to Mrs. Ponsonby!"

She sighed and rode off. There was trouble brewing, and if the antitrailer campaigners got their way, the Riverside children would be made to feel even less welcome than before!

Six

By Thursday afternoon, Mrs. Ponsonby, Mr. Western, and Mrs. Parker Smythe had succeeded in rousing half the village into a state of outrage over a few broken flowerpots.

"Poor Walter Pickard!" Mrs. Ponsonby wailed, buying her daily ration of mint toffees from McFarlanes'. "He cherished those geraniums!" Mandy caught the gist of her remarks through the open door of the post office. She was mailing letters for her grandma before she headed home to help in the clinic.

"It should never have been allowed in the first place!" she heard Mrs. Parker Smythe tell Reverend Hadcroft.

Mandy arrived home and propped her bike against the clinic wall, then went into reception. Mrs. Parker Smythe and her daughter, Imogen, were coming out, as Reverend Hadcroft went in with his cat, Jemima.

"I don't mean to be uncharitable, Reverend, far from it, but I *knew* the trailer site would mean trouble for the village. Why, only this morning I saw a whole horde of those children race past our house on those mountain bike things. And the two leaders are almost as bad as the children. They couldn't keep control of a kindergarten, never mind a bunch of unruly teenagers!" Mrs. Parker Smythe was hard to ignore, in her brilliant turquoise dress and gold jewelry.

Mandy saw Imogen sigh and hold tighter to the cardboard box containing her twin rabbits, Button and Barney.

Reverend Hadcroft smiled back. "I'm not sure that *control* is what it's all about, Mrs. Parker Smythe. After all, the children have come to Welford on vacation. They're bound to let their hair down."

"Oh, so you call destroying an old man's prize geraniums letting their hair down?" Mrs. Parker Smythe retorted. She turned and seized the attention of Mrs. Platt, who happened to be walking up to the clinic with her miniature poodle, Antonia. "Did you hear the news, Mrs. Platt? The trailer children were let loose on their bicycles up on the moor near High Cross. No thought of sticking to public roads, mind you. Oh, no, Sam Western had to threaten them with his dogs unless they kept off his land!"

Mrs. Platt looked worried. "Things seem to be getting out of hand. I must warn Vicki and Justin. They're staying with me for a few days while their mom and dad are away, and I want to keep them out of trouble. You can't be too careful with young people these days."

Mandy realized that Mrs. Platt was the Simpson twins' great-aunt. She lived in a bungalow in a small housing development and occasionally had Justin and Vicki to stay over.

She watched Reverend Hadcroft ease his way past and stopped for a moment longer to listen as the two women gossiped on.

"I felt so sorry for old Walter," Mrs. Platt went on. "I saw him sitting on his bench outside the pub last night, poor chap, and he didn't look at all like his usual cheerful self."

Mandy had heard enough. She gave Imogen a smile and went inside. Her mind was still on the thorny problem of the Riverside children as she put on her white coat and went to help her dad with the minister's cat.

"Ah, Mandy, I've already sedated Jemima, and now we just need to take a quick X ray," Dr. Adam said. "Lift her into position so we can take a picture of her tail; that's right. It looks as if she's done some serious damage to it, I'm afraid."

The minister looked on anxiously as they carried out the X ray on poor Jemima. "I noticed her tail was drooping as soon as she came in this lunchtime. She wasn't her usual self at all, so I brought her straight here."

"Quite right." Adam Hope took the plate out of the machine a few minutes later. "Look, Mandy, can you see a hairline crack across the vertebra here? About three inches from the tip? It's a fracture."

Mandy looked hard at the X ray, then nodded.

"It looks like Jemima may just have used up one of her nine lives," Dr. Adam told the minister. "She's had a narrow escape, by the look of things."

"What will you do?" He stroked his cat and whispered gently to her as she began to raise her head and look around. The sedative was wearing off.

"We'll have to perform a minor operation to remove the tip of the tail. The fracture has paralyzed the nerve supply. But don't worry, cats manage perfectly well without their tails. In fact, she probably won't even notice after a day or two." Dr. Adam picked her up and gave her to Mandy. "We'll keep her in overnight and do the job in the morning, okay?" He told Mandy to take the cat into the residential unit and make sure she was put safely inside one of the cages.

Mandy gave Jemima five-star treatment. She put an extra padding of newspaper around the base of a clean cage to stop her from banging the useless tip of her tail. She made sure she was warm and settled. By the time Mandy got back to the treatment room, Dr. Adam had seen his last patient, and surgery was finished.

Now she had time to consider what to do about the Riverside problem. She told her dad about it. "Do you think they're going around deliberately upsetting people?"

"Do *you*?"

Mandy shook her head. "I think forgetting to shut Mr. Western's gate must have been a mistake, pure and simple."

"And what about Walter's flowerpots?"

She paused. "I think the Riverside crowd is innocent until proven guilty," she decided. "I can't see that there's any concrete evidence against them!"

Her dad smiled. "Have you thought about becoming a lawyer when you grow up?"

Mandy laughed. "Oh, no, thanks. Give me animals any day!" She wanted to be a vet, like her parents. "I think I'll just pop down to James's to see what he thinks." She took off her white coat. "And to see Henry, of course!"

"Of course. How's his diet plan going?"

"Pretty good. His weight's down to four and a half ounces. James weighs him every morning on the kitchen scale!"

"Excellent. Keep up the good work!"

She went off with a smile and a wave, thinking hard about how they could help Sonia, Marcie, Ben, Paul, and the rest.

"What's up?" James asked. He'd been building Henry a playpen on the lawn out of four long planks and four bricks. The planks formed a square, propped in position and held upright by the bricks. It gave Henry a large, safe exercise area. He frolicked inside it as Mandy came into the garden.

"Mrs. Ponsonby and Mrs. Parker Smythe; that's what's up!" She flung herself onto the grass. "They're dead set on blaming the Riverside kids for every single thing that goes wrong around here!" She told him the latest mishap with Walter's geraniums. "I wish Mrs. Ponsonby wouldn't jump to conclusions," she complained. "And I wish Mr. Western wouldn't set his guard dogs on trespassers. People might not know they're on private property."

James nodded. "Have you seen anyone at Riverside today?"

"Not yet. I think most of them went mountain biking again. Has Leanne come by?"

"I don't think so. I want to show her Henry's new play area. What do you think?"

"Great!" Mandy began to smile. "And by the look of it, Henry thinks so, too!" The hamster was scampering from corner to corner, then sitting on his haunches and combing his whiskers. "And I think he's actually *looking* thinner, James! You're getting him into really good shape!"

James smiled proudly. "The extra exercise will help, too." He took a plastic dish full of clean water and placed it inside the playpen. Henry twitched his nose, bent his head, and trotted to the dish. "Just keep an eye on Henry, will you, Mandy? I want to go inside and get a bit of hard-boiled egg. He loves it."

Mandy lay full length on the warm grass, propping her chin in her hands as James went off for Henry's healthy snack. His yard was lovely and peaceful. She could hear the bees buzzing from flower to flower, birds singing in the trees overhead. Lazily she gazed at the hamster as he explored the lawn for grubs and insects.

She looked up when she heard a faint new sound coming from behind the high hedge. Voices yelled, short and sharp. Someone or something came running along the lane in the afternoon heat. The footsteps grew nearer. Mandy peered through the hedge and caught a glimpse of a striped blue-and-white T-shirt. She raised herself to her knees to see who it could be.

The figure stopped running just outside James's yard. Mandy heard someone quietly sobbing, and then she saw a girl's face looking back at her through the green hedge. When she saw she was being watched, the girl backed off and disappeared.

Footsteps started up again, heading across the road, then rustling through long grass toward a small woods opposite James's house. But Mandy had seen a flash of flaming red hair, and she guessed that the pale face and sobs belonged to Leanne. She sprang to her feet to follow her.

Out in the lane, as she checked the road for cars, Mandy spied two more figures heading toward her. She recognized Justin and Vicki Simpson, the twins from school. They were walking Antonia, their aunt's poodle, but when they saw Mandy they hesitated.

Mandy frowned. From the grins on the faces of the pair, she guessed they were the ones who'd upset Leanne and sent her crying into the woods. By now, her blue-and-white T-shirt had vanished between the slender trunks of the larch trees, so Mandy turned to wait.

"Hi, Mandy." Justin chewed the juicy end of a grass stalk and slouched along, hands in his pockets. Vicki was letting the poodle strain at the leash. The little dog was panting and pulling in the heat. "We wanted to look in on old Henry."

"Feel free." She cast a worried glance after Leanne. "He's on the lawn." She met Vicki's unblinking gaze. "James has just gone inside to get him a snack. Don't let Henry out of his playpen, will you?"

Vicki tossed her head. Her short brown hair swung back. Her solid, sunburned arm reached out and pushed open the gate to James's yard. "As if!" she retorted. Then she carelessly let go of Antonia's leash and the dog scampered across the grass toward the hamster's playpen. She had her nose to the ground and dragged the red leather leash behind.

"Watch out!" Mandy shouted a warning to James, who had just come out onto the porch with Henry's snack. James looked up, then leaped down the steps to head Antonia off. The poodle yapped. Blackie, shut up in the kitchen while Henry was out to play, set up a frenzied racket. Eric, snoozing on the mat, stood up, arched his back, and hissed.

James zipped across the lawn like lightning. He scooped Henry out of danger just as Antonia bounded into the middle of the playpen. Vicki charged after her, knocking planks down as she seized the runaway's leash. Meanwhile, Mandy fumed at Justin, who stood propped against the gate, doubled up with laughter.

"It's not funny!" Mandy protested. "And neither is upsetting Leanne Jackson. What did you say to her?" If she'd stopped to think things through, she probably wouldn't have challenged Justin, who liked putting people down whenever he had the chance.

"Oo-oh!" he replied. "No need to get upset!" He stood free of the gate. "We're touchy all of a sudden, aren't we?"

Mandy swallowed hard. "No, I'm not. I just think we should give the Riverside kids a chance to enjoy themselves. Everyone picks on them as if they were criminals or something!" Her eyes blazed. By now Antonia's yapping had died down and Vicki had firm hold of the leash. She wanted to stroke the hamster, so James held him out for inspection. Henry seemed none the worse for his close shave.

"Well, according to my aunt, that's just what they are, a bunch of vandals," Justin sneered. "It's all she's talked about since we first got here. They wrecked a whole lot of old plant pots, didn't they? And she says she bets the kids that come next week won't be any better, or the ones the week after that." He seemed to enjoy the idea of other people getting into trouble. His lazy, lip-curling grin spread from ear to ear as he sauntered across the lawn toward his sister.

Mandy was still furious. She couldn't trust herself to stick around any longer. So she cut off across the lane toward the woods, knowing that now there was little chance of tracking down Leanne.

Sure enough, the sun filtered through the spiky, bright green leaves of the larch trees, the sweet-smelling ground was soft and silent in the shadows, but Leanne had disappeared.

Seven

"Let's take Henry for a little walk," James suggested that evening.

Mandy had been staring into space. She sat on James's yard swing with the hamster asleep on her lap, but she jumped at the idea. "Down to Riverside," she suggested. Henry woke up and shook his whiskers. He blinked sleepily in the evening sunlight. "We could see if we can find Leanne and let her have a chat with Henry."

The memory of the red-haired girl slipping away into the woods, her face pale and tearstained, refused to fade from Mandy's mind. After the first, friendly visit, when Leanne had left the others playing soccer and come with Mandy to meet the hamster, they hadn't seen as much of her as they'd hoped. The shy girl had popped in once or twice with healthy treats for Henry, but the village gossip seemed to have affected her badly. She seemed to want to hide whenever Mandy saw her in the village or strolling by the river. She still looked lonely and unhappy, and now this episode with the Simpson twins had probably made things worse. "I wonder what they said to her," she muttered, lifting Henry and easing him into his cage.

James locked it securely. "Who?"

"The twins. To Leanne. I'm sure they upset her." She told him about the running footsteps and the sobbing.

"Leave it to them!" James lifted Henry's cage and together they set off for the trailer site. "Is that what's been on your mind?"

Mandy nodded. "I suppose so." They crossed the road and cut diagonally across the field toward Riverside. "It's bad enough Leanne feeling she doesn't fit in with the Kingsmill crowd, without coming here on vacation and being treated like this!"

James agreed. "Let's hope Henry will be able to cheer her up a bit." They climbed over a drystone wall into the field where the gleaming white trailers stood.

Chrissie Searle was the first to wave a friendly greeting. "Hi, I'm just going to Walton for barbecue bricks," she told them. "We're having a party tomorrow night. Would you like to come?" She stood, one foot on the minibus step, ready to haul herself up onto the driver's seat. In the space of a week, the sun had lightened her short blond hair and tanned her long limbs. She gave them a quick grin. "If you're still willing to associate with the likes of us, that is!"

Mandy grinned back. "Just try and stop us!"

"Good. Seven-thirty tomorrow evening, then!" Chrissie climbed up and started the engine. "See you there."

The minibus drove off and Pete Searle came out of the camp store. He strolled across, followed by a few of the children. Soon Mandy, James, and Henry were part of the crowd. Marcie handed around her bag of chips. Paul produced his soccer ball and began a game, while Sonia settled down and told Mandy a tale of being woken in the middle of the night.

"It was pitch-black, honest!"

Mandy sat on the grass with Henry safe inside his cage, ready to listen.

"The dead of night. I wake up, and there's this *bump-bump-bump* noise right outside the trailer!" Sonia's gray eyes widened as she told her story, and her voice dropped to a whisper. "I was scared to death, I can tell you! I dig Marcie in the ribs to wake her up. Leanne's already sitting up in bed wide awake.

"This thing, whatever it is, is going *bump-bump-bump* and the whole trailer starts to rock. I stuff the pillow in my mouth to stop myself from screaming. Even Marcie closes her eyes and clings to me.

"But Leanne just gets out of bed, goes across, and flings open the door like it's broad daylight out there! There are these huge, white, rolling eyes staring in at us. I think I'm going to faint. But Leanne starts saying, 'There, there,' and making these clicking noises with her tongue. By this time I've got my hands over my eyes and I can hardly breathe, I'm so scared. But when I take a peek, there's Leanne going for sugar cubes in the bowl and handing them to this enormous thing that's snorting and breathing all over us. He's halfway up the steps by now!"

Mandy burst out laughing. "What was it?"

"A giant horse! Gray. Well, sort of ghostly white in the moonlight. Apparently it had got in from the next field. But Leanne didn't turn a hair. She stroked its neck and talked nicely to it. Then she went off to take it safely back to its field. And the thing is, when she came back she was actually looking happy, like she'd enjoyed the whole thing!"

"Where is she now?" Mandy looked around, beyond the noisy game of soccer, toward the river.

"Who, Leanne? Don't ask me. She's probably wandered off somewhere by herself again. It's a pity, really. Me and Marcie, we think she's okay, only she's hard to get to know, she really is." Sonia glanced down toward the riverbank and spotted something. "Oh, there she is, daydreaming as usual."

Mandy smiled and stood up, took Henry's cage, and headed quietly for the river, as Sonia turned her face to the sun, ready for a bit of sunbathing.

Mandy didn't say anything as she sat down beside Leanne, who just gazed at the water that swirled lazily at her feet. Instead, she took Henry from his cage and settled him on her own lap. She began to tickle his ears with a blade of grass and waited for her friend to respond. Eventually, Leanne's gaze swiveled sideways.

"Hi, Mandy. Hi, Henry." Leanne's low voice ended in a sigh.

"Hi." Mandy handed over the hamster. "Don't you think he's lost weight? James's diet is working really well." She was careful not to mention the episode with Justin and Vicki earlier that day.

Leanne drew Henry to eye level in the palm of her

hand. She nestled him close against her cheek. "Yes, and he's still so soft!"

"And his coat is really shiny now!" Mandy agreed. "That's because of the exercise and a better diet. We cut out all the starchy snacks that the kids used to give him at school."

Leanne sighed again. She handed Henry back to Mandy and drew her knees under her chin.

"I have to go home the day after tomorrow."

"I know. Will you be glad?"

"In one way. I'm looking forward to seeing my mom. But I won't see Henry anymore, will I?"

Mandy hesitated. "You could come back and see him," she offered. "Whenever you want."

But Leanne turned away. "I don't think so, Mandy."

"Oh, don't mind what some people around here are saying!" Mandy wanted to put the record straight. "Take no notice of the likes of Justin and Vicki. Whatever they say, we think it's great having you here, me and James, that is. And my mom and dad, and my grandparents. And James's family. We all like having the trailers in the village!"

A brief smile flitted across Leanne's thin face. "But you haven't heard the latest, have you?"

"No, what?" Mandy stroked Henry and put him in his cage for a rest.

"Well, you know the tennis courts?"

Mandy nodded. "Just over there." She pointed to an area a couple of hundred yards upriver.

"There's a few new trees planted along by the river-bank."

"I know." Mandy pictured the saplings, carefully supported by thick wooden stakes and protected by a slim plastic tube around their trunks.

"Well, someone went along and snapped two of them

clean in half. For no reason. No one saw it happen, but guess who got the blame?" Leanne turned to Mandy, her eyes full of anger. "No, you don't need to say it out loud!"

Mandy groaned. "Not again!"

"See? Whatever goes wrong around here, we get the blame for it. And those twins enjoyed rubbing my nose in it!"

"This afternoon?"

Leanne nodded. "I was just walking down to James's house when they saw me and stopped me. Then, when they found out where I was from, they started yelling and calling me names."

"What did they say?" Mandy went to stand at the water's edge. She felt ashamed and angry at the same time.

"All sorts of things. They called us vandals and stuff like that. They said to go back to the city where we belonged. And they said everyone around here hates us!"

"Well, we don't!" Mandy was steadfast. She tried to think straight. "Anything could've happened to those trees. Just like Walter's flowerpots! I'll go home and ask Grandpa; he knows all about what happens down at the tennis courts!"

Leanne tried to smile. "Thanks, Mandy. But it's too late."

"No, it's not. We'll get to the bottom of what's going on around here," she promised.

"I hope you do. But what I mean is, it's too late for us. Too late for me. I can't come back to Welford and visit, see. Not after a week like this. I wouldn't ever dare to show my face again!"

Mandy poked the toe of her sneaker into the clear water. "Do you all think like that? Marcie, Sonia, Paul, and the rest?"

"Pretty much. Look, it's not your fault. Just forget it, Mandy." Leanne stood up and ran a hand through her red hair, pushing it clear of her face. "I only hope the kids who come to Riverside after us get along better with the people in the village. Maybe it's just our bunch that they don't like."

"I doubt it." Mandy shook her head, thinking of the fuss that Mr. Western, Mrs. Ponsonby, and Mrs. Parker Smythe would be making over the latest "proof" against the trailer kids.

"Well." Leanne shrugged and turned to go. Then she remembered Henry and stooped to peek into his cage. "Bye, Henry," she whispered.

Henry twitched his little nose and blinked. He ran to the front of his cage to peer back.

"Do you think he knows I'm saying good-bye?"

Leanne asked as she turned away, her eyes brimming with tears.

Mandy couldn't bring herself to answer. She watched as Leanne walked off toward her trailer, her own eyes filling with tears at the sadness and injustice of it all.

Eight

"Not a very good day for a barbecue," Grandma commented when she dropped in on Animal Ark the following morning. The sky had turned cloudy overnight, and a soft drizzle had begun to fall.

"Not a very good day at all!" Mandy stood in reception. She was wearing her white vet's coat and an unusually downhearted expression. The clinic wasn't due to open for half an hour, so Mandy was keeping herself busy by tidying Jean Knox's desk.

"Why, what's the matter?" Grandma bustled up the steps and put her shopping basket on a chair in the waiting room. "This isn't like you, Mandy dear." She smiled a greeting at her son, Adam Hope, already at work in one of the treatment rooms. He was getting Jemima ready to go home after the successful operation on her tail.

"Hello there, Mom." He came out. "What brings you here? I was going to say bright and early, but it isn't really, is it?"

"Apparently not." Grandma was puzzled by the dull atmosphere. She looked curiously at her son.

"No use rolling your eyes and raising your eyebrows, Mom." Mandy's dad came out with it straight. "Why don't you get Mandy to tell you the latest episode in the Riverside soap opera? It's on daily, you know. It looks like you missed the latest dramatic installment!"

"Ah!" Grandma seemed to see the light. "You mean the broken trees? Oh, yes, I heard about that. As a matter of fact, Tom is down at the tennis courts right this moment, taking a look." To make herself useful, she joined Mandy at the desk and began to sort out leaflets about booster injections against cat flu and other common ailments.

When the phone rang, Grandma quickly picked it up. "It's for you," she said to Mandy, handing it over. "Your mom's put the call through from the house."

"Hello?" Mandy wasn't expecting a call.

"Hello." A small voice spoke, then hesitated. "This is Imogen."

"Hi, Imogen!" She tried to hide her surprise. "There isn't something the matter with Button or Barney, is there?" She couldn't think why else Imogen Parker Smythe would want to get in touch.

"No, it's not that. It's just that I wanted to say I was sorry."

"What about?" Mandy gave her grandmother a puzzled frown.

"About my mom writing to the council people again with that long list of names."

"The petition!" Mandy's voice rose. "You mean they've actually sent it?"

"This morning. Does that mean the trailers will have to leave?" Imogen sounded upset. "People don't like the trailer children, do they?"

"*Some* people don't," Mandy agreed. "But thanks for telling me, Imogen." There was another long pause. "There isn't anything else, is there?" She suspected there was something else on Imogen's mind.

"No. Yes! That is, can you come to my house?" The trembling voice sounded tearful. "I need to tell you something else; a secret. But I can't say it on the phone."

"All right, I'll try to later on," Mandy promised. But her mind was on the petition. It seemed Mr. Western, Mrs. Ponsonby, and Imogen's mom were really determined to get rid of the trailers at last. "Bye," she said absentmindedly, and she put the phone down.

"It looks like they're going to win," she told her grandmother. "I bet they've been collecting signatures all week. And now they'll say they've got proper evidence!"

Dr. Adam snorted and retired to his treatment room. "Evidence!"

"I bet they've told the council about the flowerpots, the cows on the loose up in the field, and now the broken trees," Mandy continued. "They'll say permission for the trailer site should be withdrawn because of all the trouble the city kids have caused."

Grandma's tongue tut-tutted rapidly. "Well, really!"

"It's not fair, is it, Grandma?"

"It certainly is not!" She tapped the sheaf of leaflets smartly against the desk. "From what Tom says, it doesn't seem likely that even superhuman children could have broken those saplings. He says they were probably too strong to be snapped off like that."

"Exactly!" Mandy agreed.

"That's why he wanted to take a look for himself."

"Now, there's no point in you two just guessing," Dr.

Adam warned from the other room. "That would make you as bad as Sam Western's lot!"

"No way!" Mandy was annoyed. "This isn't *guessing*, Dad!" Her fighting spirit was on the mend after her chat with Grandma. "Take the flowerpots; anyone coming out of the pub could've got into their car and backed into them!"

"Without even realizing." Grandma was ready to back her up. "Look, dear, what you must do now is follow up these theories. If you really want to help your friends at the trailer site, that is."

"You're right, Grandma!" With her head high and a determined look on her face, she went into the treatment room. "Dad, you don't need me for the clinic this morning, do you?"

"No. Jemima here is ready for Reverend Hadcroft to pick up. And Simon's due at any moment. There aren't many appointments in the book, I don't think. Why?" His eyes twinkled at her.

"You know why! I want to go and see Grandpa. Then I want to go up to Beacon House to see Imogen. I think she might have something important to tell me. Then after that, I don't know what I'll do. It depends on what happens."

"What happens with what?" He played dumb, his head to one side.

"With my investigations! I intend to find out the real people behind all this damage!" she said in a strong, clear voice. "It's wrong for Riverside to get all the blame. It'll ruin everything for the kids who are supposed to come here for their vacation this summer."

"That's my girl!" A smile spread across Dr. Adam's face as he gave her a quick hug.

Mandy grinned back and took off her white coat. "Thanks, Grandma," she said as she hung it on its hook. And without waiting for any more advice, she ran outside for her bike and pedaled swiftly down to the tennis courts.

Grandpa stood in the drizzle, hunched up in his green padded jacket. He stared thoughtfully at the two snapped saplings. The cruel, jagged ends showed up pale through the mist. He looked up as Mandy ran to greet him.

"Hello, where's your jacket, love?" he asked, casting an eye at the heavy clouds. "And what brings you down here?"

"I was looking for you, Grandpa." She tramped through the long grass. Behind her, the immaculate grass courts stretched, smooth as pool tables. "I wanted to know what you think. Did kids do this?" She went and peered closely at the damaged trees.

Slowly Grandpa shook his head. "Do you want my expert opinion, love?"

She nodded eagerly. Her grandpa knew everything there was to know about plants and gardening. He would know how hard it was to snap these trees.

"Well, I'd say it was impossible to do that with bare hands."

Mandy took a sharp breath. "Oh, Grandpa!"

"I mean it. Just imagine, if you ever tried to get rid of a strong shoot that you didn't want growing in your garden — a bramble or a stray sycamore. Well, it takes all your strength to snap something like that, and these two trees here are a good bit thicker than that."

Mandy pushed a stray, wet strand of hair from her forehead. "So what do you think could have done it?"

Grandpa stooped to examine the ruined trunks. He sighed. "That's harder to say. But look here, this plastic tube that protected the tree is split right down to the bottom, and there are scratches along the bark. I'd say that it was done by some sort of machine with sharp edges." He stood up straight and looked up and down the riverbank, as if the machine could still be spotted there.

"A machine? What sort of machine?"

"Who knows? But if you think about it, it has to be a Land Rover or a tractor or some such thing to get down here. Yes, I'd say it was something strong and heavy like that. It must have caught the trees as it passed."

"But definitely not kids?" she repeated.

"No," he said. "Definitely not."

With fresh hope in her heart, Mandy waved good-bye to her grandpa and shot off again on her bike in the direction of Beacon House. Grandpa had promised to pass on his verdict to people in the village, while Mandy raced up to visit Imogen Parker Smythe.

"It may be too late to stop the petition now," he warned. "And there are those other incidents supposedly involving the Riverside children, remember!"

But Mandy refused to be downcast. As she cycled up the long hill, her legs aching, her chest heaving, she felt sure that this next visit would be another step toward clearing their name. After all, Imogen's phone call had come out of the blue. And she'd sounded shaky, as if something was bothering her.

Mandy arrived at last and found the security gates open and a black car standing in the driveway. She cycled straight up to the front door of Beacon House, then rang the bell, glad to see Imogen's dad and not her mom come through the hall to answer it.

He opened the door. "Hello," Mr. Parker Smythe said, surprised by Mandy's damp and disheveled appearance. "Have you come to see Immi?" He stood in a bright green golf sweater, one hand on the door, holding it half open. Imogen herself came bounding downstairs two at a time. "Mandy's come to play!" she shouted, slipping in between her tall father and the door. "I invited her!" She dragged Mandy by the arm into the tiled hallway and straight upstairs. At seven years old, she was small but chubby and strong. Mandy felt herself being propelled into Imogen's splendid bedroom, complete with television, phone, bathroom, and cuddly toys.

Quickly Imogen pushed the door closed. "Oh, good, you came!" she gasped, still refusing to let go of Mandy's arm.

Mandy stared at her red cheeks and secretive expression. "Are you okay?" She felt herself plumped down on the embroidered white comforter on Imogen's soft bed. A giant black-and-white panda and a pink teddy bear toppled from the banked-up pillows and fell into her lap.

"Yes! No! Oh, dear!" Imogen, too, collapsed on the bed, half in tears. "I've got something to tell you, only Mommy will be angry with me if I do." She bit her lip and turned away. "I wish I'd told someone sooner, then they wouldn't have got into all this trouble!"

"Who? Who wouldn't have got into trouble?" Mandy tried to calm her down by speaking quietly.

"Those trailer children. They're going to be sent

away, aren't they? The trailers, I mean. And all because of the flowerpots. And Mommy says they deserve it, and it's my fault because I let her think it was them, and then it was too late!" Imogen wailed and buried her face in her hands.

'Too late?" Mandy repeated. "No, it's not too late, Imogen. You can tell me what really happened. You know, don't you?"

Miserably the little girl looked up and nodded. "I saw. Mommy was in the post office buying a newspaper. I stayed in the car." She paused.

"Go on," Mandy said quietly. "You see, it isn't fair to let someone else take the blame when it's not their fault. You wouldn't like it, would you?"

Imogen shook her head. "I never noticed the flower-pots at first. I was looking at the cat."

"Which cat?"

"Mr. Pickard's big tomcat. He was sitting on the wall in the sun."

Mandy nodded. "That must have been Tom. Then what?"

"Next thing, the little poodle came running up to him. She jumped up. Tom hissed, and the dog jumped higher and higher, till it crashed into a flowerpot. She sent them all crashing down. Tom ran off and the dog stopped barking. When Mommy came out of the shop, they'd both run away. All the flowers were on the ground and the pots were broken!"

Mandy took a deep breath. "And your mom didn't notice there was anything wrong?"

Again Imogen shook her head.

"Do you know whose dog it was?"

"It was a little white dog with a red collar. They shouted out its name. They called her Antonia, but she never took any notice!"

"Who's they? Who called?" Mandy frowned. These unknown people had witnessed the accident along with Imogen, but they, too, had kept quiet about it ever since. She felt herself grow hot and angry.

"I don't know. It was a big girl and boy. They both looked the same. I think they must have been twins," Imogen trailed off tearfully. "Mommy drove away, and I never said anything because I thought the big boy and girl would get into trouble. And then . . . and then, everyone said it was the trailer children, and it was too late!" Imogen started crying in earnest.

"Vicki and Justin Simpson!" Mandy let the truth sink in. Then she stood up, freeing herself from Imogen. She felt a small surge of victory; here was the first real proof that the Riverside children were innocent!

She went straight out and found Mr. Parker Smythe

still hovering at the bottom of the stairs. Mandy explained why Imogen was upset. He listened and nodded, then quickly took charge.

"I don't know much about this petition," he confessed. "I've been away on business for most of this week. But from what you say, it seems I'd better tell my wife what really happened to the flowerpots. It puts a whole new light on things. Leave it to me. I'll see what I can do," he promised.

"Will you please tell Mr. Western and Mrs. Ponsonby, too?" Mandy felt that things were working out well. Now she longed to race down to Riverside and tell them about the progress they'd made; the city visitors were in the clear over breaking the flowerpots and the trees.

"Of course." He nodded kindly.

"And tell Imogen thanks from me, would you?" Mandy headed for the door. "And ask her if she'd like to come to the barbecue this evening. She can come and join in the celebration, since all's well!"

Then she was off, down the long driveway, under the oak trees. She jumped on her bike, sped down the twisting road, through the village as the clouds began to lift and a watery sun shone through. She raced along the lane to the Hunters' house, brimming with excitement, hardly able to contain the good news. "James will want to come with me!" she told herself firmly, flinging open his gate.

"James!" She ran up the path. The house was shut up. There was no car in the driveway. Even Blackie was silent. Only Eric stalked across the lawn, his tail up and swishing from side to side.

That's odd, Mandy thought, halting in midstride. She spotted yellow flower heads lying scattered over the grass, and one of Mr. Hunter's flower beds had been roughly trampled. Crushed marigolds lay on the damp soil, their petals strewn far and wide.

"James!" Now Mandy ran to the side of the house, to see if anyone was there. But the doors and windows were shut. Everyone was out and alarm began to dart through her. Who had come in and trampled on the garden? Was anything else damaged? She flew back around the front of the house and stared at the lawn, then slowly she went up the bottom step onto the front porch.

"Henry?" Her voice caught in her dry throat. There was the cage on the shelf. But the top was flung open. "Oh, no!" She leaped the final two steps to look inside the cage. Henry's straw bedding was scattered loosely over the bottom, his drinking bowl had been tipped over, the sawdust was waterlogged. Even his exercise wheel lay on one side, and the ramp to his sleeping gallery had been wrenched out of position.

"Oh, Henry!" Mandy gasped. Frantically she searched every corner. But it was no good; the hamster's cage was empty. Henry had vanished.

Nine

"And you're sure you left the cage safely locked?" Mrs. Hunter repeated. She stood on the porch, trying to understand what was going on.

James was white-faced. They'd searched long and hard for Henry since they'd arrived home from shopping, but now he stood and stared at the empty cage. "Yes, I locked him in! I'm sure I did!"

"Yes, look, the lock's been forced open," Mandy said. She examined the twisted bolt. "It's not James's fault, Mrs. Hunter. Henry didn't just escape. He's been stolen!"

James's mother put down her shopping and went to let Blackie out of the back of the car. The dog bounded up the steps and began to sniff around the porch. He gave a sharp bark. Then his head went down again as he trotted out onto the lawn.

"I think he's picked up some sort of scent." Mandy tried to think straight. James's car had arrived just as she'd discovered Henry's disappearance. She had greeted them with the dreadful news and watched the color drain from her friend's face. "Blackie knows there's been an intruder, don't you, boy?" She had followed him into the garden as the dog sniffed among the scattered marigold petals and the deep footprints in the flower bed.

"But why? What's going on?" James sat heavily on the top step of the porch. He fought to control his feelings. "Mandy, what am I going to tell Miss Temple when we get back to school? I can't tell her that I lost Henry, can I?"

"You didn't," Mandy said firmly. "Henry's been taken deliberately. Whoever stole Henry made a mess of the yard as well. Now, why would anyone want to do that?" She went to where the Labrador was sniffing at the deep prints. But her thoughts whirled without order. Henry was missing. The cage was empty. The flowers were trampled. But none of it came together to make any sense.

"And that's not the only thing." Mrs. Hunter sighed as

she swung down the back door of the car. "We just drove through the village on the way back from the supermarket. There was a bit of a fuss going on outside the pub. We stopped to find out what it was about. Apparently one of the kids from the trailer site is missing. Pete Cavendish was there trying to organize a sort of search party."

James sat with his head in his hands, not reacting. But Mandy felt the hairs on the back of her neck start to prickle at the news. "Who? Who's missing?" This was the last day at Riverside for the Kingsmill children. Everyone should be getting ready for tonight's barbecue, not spending time searching for one of their party.

"I don't remember the name." Mrs. Hunter eased past James to take her shopping into the house. "Do you?" she asked him. "James, Mandy was asking who they're looking for in the village."

James looked up. "Leanne," he said quietly.

"I knew it!"

"She went off sometime this morning and she's not been seen for hours. No one saw where she went."

"Oh, no!" The prickling sensation spread down her spine. "Oh, James, you don't think Leanne . . . she couldn't have, could she?" Mandy stared over his head at Henry's empty cage.

"You mean, Leanne was feeling so bad about leaving

tomorrow and not seeing Henry again, and she was so fed up and miserable about everything that she came and stole him and ran away?"

Mandy nodded. "I'm not saying she *did*! I'm just saying she *might have*!" If you added things up, it was quite possible. She groaned. "Why couldn't she just have waited an hour or two longer?"

Still shocked by Henry's disappearance, James got slowly to his feet. "Why, what difference would that have made?"

"We could have gotten over to Riverside and told them the latest news. It turns out the Kingsmill kids had nothing to do with Walter's flowerpots getting smashed, and probably nothing to do with the broken trees, either!" Rushing through the morning's events, Mandy told James what had really gone on. "If Leanne had known that and knew that people in the village might not be so horrible to her anymore, she would never have run off like this!"

"Maybe." Mrs. Hunter came out of the house with two cups of tea. She handed one to James. "Here, I think you should drink this while I telephone your father at work. I want to discuss what we should do. I've already checked inside the house, and everything there is just as we left it. It's only the yard that's damaged, and of course, poor Henry."

She left them to mope over the defenseless little hamster; nearsighted, overfriendly Henry, with his lovely marmalade coat and twitching whiskers. Where was he now? Was somebody taking good care of him? Mandy shuddered at the thought that the kidnapper might get scared and abandon him. He could be stranded in the middle of nowhere, unable to look after himself and terrified.

"I only hope Leanne is looking after him," James said miserably. His own thoughts had tended in the same direction.

"Oh, she will!" Mandy put on a brave face. "Leanne *loves* Henry!"

"If it *was* Leanne."

"Well, they both seem to have disappeared at more or less the same time. And she knew she was never going to see Henry again; she told me she'd never come back to Welford."

There was a pause. They were at a loss, still swamped by fears for the missing hamster.

Then Mrs. Hunter came bustling back. "I phoned your dad, James. He says not to worry. We could always buy another hamster for the school."

He shook his head. "It wouldn't be the same."

"No, but your dad was only trying to be practical. For instance, he wondered what was the point of the intruder trampling through the flower bed. I must say, I find that very strange, too!"

They all wandered across the lawn together to examine the heavy footprints.

"Well, it was no accident, that's for sure," Mandy said. "Someone's great big boots have stamped over here on purpose."

"Your dad also said that if this Leanne girl is your prime suspect for Henry-napping, why don't you two go and join in the search for her? Better than standing around doing nothing."

It took Mandy only a second to agree. "Let's take Blackie," she suggested. "I'm sure he's picked up the scent. If we take him along, he can help in the search!"

So they went off down the road, with Blackie eagerly snuffling and tracking a scent. They approached Chrissie Searle, standing at the entrance to the trailer site. She was poring over an ordinance survey map and directing Marcie and Sonia toward the woods, where Leanne sometimes hung out.

She greeted them with a worried frown. "Have you heard?"

Mandy nodded. "We've come to help you look." She thought it best to keep their suspicions about Leanne and Henry to themselves.

"That's good of you, thanks." Chrissie sighed. "Poor kid, I think she's been really unhappy here."

"What do you want us to do?" James asked. He had to restrain Blackie by putting him on a short leash. "Follow the others?"

"No, I've got this side of the village more or less covered. There's no real panic just yet. She's only been gone a couple of hours. But Marcie overheard her crying late last night, and this morning no one could get a word out of her at breakfast. Then she was missing. Pete and I thought we'd better start checking things out. We've been worried about her all along. She was too much of a loner, and now it looks as if something was really bothering her."

Mandy nodded. She turned to James. "Let's run into the village, to see if there's anything we can do there."

"Good idea." Chrissie folded up her map, ready to set off up the hill after the distant figures of Ben and Paul. "You'll find Pete organizing things there. Half the village has turned out to help, much to our surprise!" With a nod, she set off along the public footpath, peering carefully to right and left as she went.

Mandy was surprised to see Mrs. Ponsonby, brightly dressed in a daffodil-yellow outfit. She was at the center of the huddle of people gathered outside the Fox and

Goose, standing beside the tall figure of Mr. Parker Smythe. Pete Cavendish, Mrs. Platt, Walter Pickard, and Ernie Bell were also listening closely.

As Mandy and James approached, they heard Mrs. Ponsonby begin to hold forth.

". . . So it seems, Walter, we may have been wrong all along!" Her rich voice rose above the murmur of all the rest. "Most unfortuante, but all too true, I'm afraid!"

Mandy stopped and stared at James.

"Sit, Blackie!" he ordered quietly. In spite of their worries about Leanne and Henry, the opportunity to hear Mrs. Ponsonby launching into a full apology was too good to miss. They hovered quietly by the side of the pub.

"If, as Mr. Parker Smythe says, there are eyewitnesses!" Mrs. Ponsonby considered things. "And of course, Mr. Parker Smythe, we would never doubt your word. No, indeed! We know very well that you always have the best interests of the village at heart!" She flattered and smiled, holding Pandora snuggled under one arm, with patient Toby sitting to heel among the crush of trouser legs and skirts.

"And I'm sorry to hear that naughty Antonia and Tom were the ones who were to blame," Mrs. Ponsonby continued. "You see, Walter, there was a teeny-weeny fight between them, and your poor geraniums became the casualties of war! A pure accident, of course. I know that little Antonia can be a teeny bit wild at times, can't she, Pandora? But I'm sure she didn't mean any real harm!"

Walter stood in his shirtsleeves, scratching his head. "Yes, well, Tom's always up to mischief. And he's never been one to back away from a fight."

Mandy peered around the corner to hear Mrs. Platt offer her own, much quieter apology. "If I'd known Antonia had had anything to do with it, or that nephew and niece of mine, I'd have come straight up the street, knocking on your door with the money to pay for the new plants," she assured him. "I'm very sorry, Walter. I really am."

"Yes, well," Walter mumbled again. "It's all water under the bridge." He took a glance at his bare wall and shook his head.

In the short silence that followed, Mandy, James, and Blackie went forward to join the group. By now Mrs. Ponsonby was gathering fresh steam. She fixed her straw hat firmly on her head and made a solemn announcement. "The truth is out, thanks to Mr. Parker Smythe's dear little girl, Imogen! And we have to be big enough to admit, each and every one of us, that we made a terrible mistake in saying that the trailer children were the cause of it all!"

"Blow me down!" Ernie Bell muttered. He gave a sly wink as he spotted Mandy.

"No!" Mrs. Ponsonby raised her free hand to beg for silence. "We must! Mr. Western, Mrs. Parker Smythe, and I simply jumped to the wrong conclusion. And I know I speak for them all when I say that we wish to make amends!"

She turned with a swish of yellow skirt to face Pete Cavendish. "To show how truly sorry we are, I can pledge that the whole village will stand by on the alert to help you in your search for the unfortunate girl. It seems she's a sensitive little soul, and our accusations may well have pushed her to the very brink before she decided to run away!" Mrs. Ponsonby's voice had taken on a low, sorrowful tone. "The very least we can do is to help to find her!"

Pete Cavendish nodded his dark, wavy head. "Thanks very much, Mrs. Ponsonby."

"Not at all. Now, first we need a description!"

"Well, Leanne is fairly small and slim. She has chin-length red hair, lots of it, and she was wearing a blue-and-white T-shirt, jeans, and sneakers." Pete filled them in on the appearance of the missing girl.

"Very good." Mrs. Ponsonby squared her shoulders. "Pass that around, everybody! Now I must go and telephone Mr. Western to inform him of the latest news.

Ernie, you come along with me to Bleakfell Hall. We must make a thorough search of the grounds, leave no stone unturned. Come along now, everyone!"

Mandy and James watched poor Ernie's face fall a mile. But there was no arguing with Mrs. Ponsonby. They watched the group disperse. Mr. Parker Smythe promised to check the field beyond Beacon House, while Walter wandered off toward the pub to rustle up more help.

"We'll head down the valley," Mandy told Pete. "I know Leanne didn't usually go down that way, toward Graystones Farm, but all the more reason to look down there, I suppose."

"You may well be right." Pete nodded his approval.

"Aren't you going to call the police?" James asked. He still had Blackie on the leash. The dog seemed upset by recent events and was being even more disobedient than usual. He was whining and straining to be off the leash.

"Not yet. If Leanne hasn't turned up by dinnertime, we'll think again. But I'd like to make a thorough search ourselves before involving anyone else. We don't want to be alarmist; in the end we might find that she just wandered off for a quiet stroll. You know what she's like." But though he sounded calm, he looked worried.

"Go on, you look downriver, like you said. We'll all meet up again at four, back at Riverside. Okay?"

Mandy and James nodded and set off. Now James could let Blackie off the leash, and he streaked ahead, down the path by Walter's cottage, toward the river. They could just see his black tail waving above the tall grass. "He seems to know where we're heading!" Mandy said. They had to run to keep him in sight. "Look, he's picking up that scent again!"

"This way, that's right, boy!" James said. They took a left turn by the edge of the clear water and headed for the square stone farmhouse in the distance where Brandon Gill and his family ran their pig farm. Blackie sniffed and was off again, loping along the pebbly shore, while Mandy and James kept to the narrow path.

Mandy seized a long stick from the bank and used it to swish aside bushes and undergrowth of poor man's orchid and willow herb. A strong aniseed perfume rose in the damp air.

"At least it's stopped raining," James said. "That's something, I suppose." Then he drew to a sudden halt. "Shh! Here, Blackie! Here, boy!"

Mandy halted, too, while the dog charged ahead regardless. "What is it?"

"I spotted something." James crouched and peered

through some bushes toward a clearing about fifty yards ahead.

"Yes!" Mandy saw a patch of blue, then red. "Two people!" She saw Blackie race into the clearing, barking frantically. She stood up and sighed. "Well, no chance of sneaking up on them, whoever it is. What's got into Blackie? I've never seen him as disobedient as this!"

James shook his head. They heard a boy's voice call. "All right, James Hunter, we know you're there! Come out, come out, wherever you are!" The voice mocked them. Mandy recognized the jeering tone of Justin Simpson.

"Oh, no!" This was the last person she wanted to meet.

"Can't you keep your dog under control?" he taunted, as James and Mandy emerged into the clearing.

"You should talk!" Mandy retorted. She felt herself blush, as she mumbled a quick hello to Brandon and confronted Justin. It was Justin's red shirt that she'd spotted, and he stood now, swinging his foot at Blackie, who had crouched, alert and growling, just out of reach.

"What are you talking about?" Justin hooked his thumbs into his belt and tried to outstare Mandy.

"I mean, *you* can't even keep your aunt's poodle under control!" she said angrily. She hated to see anyone trying to use their feet against an animal.

He realized in a flash what she meant and turned to avoid her gaze. "Who told you about that?"

"Never mind. But we know it was you and Vicki who let Antonia have that fight with old Tom. Those flower-pots were your fault!"

"Says who?" Justin bluffed, then resorted to insult. "You're a great pair of little detectives, aren't you?" he sneered.

"Now hang on a minute," Brandon cut in. "No need to

be nasty, Justin!" He looked puzzled. "What's up with Blackie, James? He isn't usually like this."

The dog had crouched low, ready to leap forward at James's command. He growled and glared at Justin.

But now Mandy stopped dead in her tracks. She forgot the flowerpots. She forgot Antonia and Tom. Her mind was focused on something completely new. "Sneakers!" she said in a faint whisper.

"What?" James held onto Blackie's collar and tried to calm him. "What on earth are you talking about, Mandy?"

"Sneakers! Remember, Pete said Leanne was wearing a blue-and-white top, jeans, and *sneakers*!"

"So?" James held on tight to Blackie. Justin stood his ground, feet planted wide apart, while Brandon frowned in bewilderment.

"It wasn't sneakers that made those footprints in your garden, James! It was a pair of heavy boots!" She stared at Justin's feet. That was what had done it; she'd noticed the mud caked to his black boots as he swung out at Blackie. "It wasn't Leanne after all!"

The sound of her voice, breathless and scared, set Blackie off again. He barked and strained against James, snarling at Justin, who still braved it out. Behind the bravado, Mandy thought she saw a flicker of real fear.

"Just what are you trying to prove?" Justin demanded. He laughed and jerked his head back in contempt.

But Mandy's mind was made up. Justin was mixed up in this somehow. That was why Blackie had flown at him; the dog had followed his scent all the way from the yard to this clearing. Justin Simpson was the one who'd trampled the flowers. And there was mud on the patterned sole of his heavy boots to prove it.

"Where's Vicki, Justin?" she whispered. Her gaze flicked sideways to the gnarled and twisted trunks of the hawthorns at the far side of the clearing.

"Not here. Why?"

If Justin was involved, Vicki was seldom far away. Mandy turned to stare at him again through narrowed eyes.

"Okay. So where's Henry?" She met his angry gaze. She managed to speak calmly.

Justin snorted, then laughed. "Are you crazy? That's it, you're around the bend, Mandy Hope!" He lunged at her, but Brandon held him off.

"Calm down!"

Justin wrenched free. "Lay off, Brandon! Keep out of this! And you'd better not go spreading rumors about me and my sister!" he yelled at Mandy. "You can't prove a thing, and I'll say you're crazy! I'll say you set that dog onto me, Hunter! I'll tell everyone it's mad and dangerous!" Justin glared as he backed off from Blackie. Then he bent to seize a rough stone the size of his fist. He flung it at Blackie, missing his head by inches.

This time, Brandon flung himself at the dog to stop him from launching himself at the enemy. "*You're* the crazy idiot around here!" he yelled at Justin.

Justin laughed as he scrambled up the bank between the trees. Then he vaulted a wall, out of sight.

"Quick!" Mandy ran and grabbed James by the arm. "Come on, you two," she said. "We've got to find Vicki before he does!"

"Why? What's going on around here?" Brandon demanded. He stroked Blackie's soft black nose to calm him down.

"Vicki's the one who took Henry!" Mandy cried. "I'm certain of it! Come on, you two, let's try Mrs. Platt's house. We've got to get there first, or who knows what they'll do to him!"

Ten

"Yes," Mrs. Platt admitted. Her face was creased into a worried frown. "Yes, as a matter of fact, I think Vicki did have a little hamster in her room. I couldn't think where it had come from, but before I could ask her about it, Justin came back home!"

Mandy stood on the doorstep of Mrs. Platt's small, neat bungalow, nodding breathlessly. "When was that, Mrs. Platt? Can you tell me how long ago Justin arrived?"

The twins' mild-mannered great-aunt thought for a moment that seemed to stretch to an age. Please be quick, Mandy thought. She had more questions jostling for position as she waited for Mrs. Platt's reply.

"Not long ago. A few minutes, that's all. It seemed as if he was in an almighty hurry, banging doors and charging around."

"And you say that he and Vicki went straight out again?"

"Yes. He dashed into her room with something urgent to tell her, I expect. Before I had time to turn around they were both racing out the front door. I could hear Antonia barking out in the street. They didn't even bother to fasten the front gate!"

"Did Vicki take Henry, I mean, the hamster, with her? Did you notice?"

Again Mrs. Platt nodded, then frowned. "Oh, dear, I'm afraid they've got themselves into more trouble, haven't they?"

Mandy didn't reply. Justin had beaten them to it after all. He must have cut across country from Brandon's place, across the farmers' fields, to reach the village before them. "Do you know where they were going, Mrs. Platt?"

"Oh, no, dear. They didn't tell me. They were in far too much of a hurry." Mrs. Platt kept an eye on Antonia, who trotted down the path to greet Blackie. James and

Brandon were waiting with him at the gate. Suddenly, she looked at them aghast. "You don't mean to say that you think Vicki *stole* the hamster? Oh, no!"

Mandy nodded. "That's what it looks like. Did you see which way they went?" By now, her heart was in her mouth. Justin must have told Vicki that they'd been found out. Now they were both out there with Henry and probably about to do something desperate.

"Oh, dear, now wait a minute. Yes, they went that way!" Mrs. Platt waved her hand toward the main street, past the pub and the church, toward Riverside. "When I went out to bring Antonia back in I spotted them heading up the road toward the trailer site!"

"Thanks!" Mandy gasped. She turned and ran down the path. "They're heading for Riverside!" she told James and Brandon. "And they've got Henry! Come on, we'd better hurry!"

Straining every muscle to catch up with the culprits, the three of them raced the length of the village street. James let Blackie run ahead. When he came to the sign for Riverside, the Labrador darted sideways through the gate.

"That's it, good boy!" James cried. "Where are they, Blackie? Go on, boy, fetch!"

Eager as ever, Blackie wove between the new trail-

ers. The site looked deserted; everyone was out combing the area, looking for Leanne, so Blackie's busy nose
wasn't distracted by other scents.

"Why would the twins head this way?" Brandon wondered. He paused to catch his breath just outside the
camp store.

James bent forward to ease a stitch in his side. "I
don't know. But you can bet your life that Blackie
knows what he's doing. They've got to be around here
somewhere!"

Meanwhile, Mandy went ahead, following on Blackie's
heels, praying that he was on the right track. "Go on,
boy, find them!" She dropped onto her hands and knees
to peer into the gloom under one of the trailers, then
she backed out. Blackie had squeezed through to the
other side and was off again, nose to the ground, tail
wagging urgently for her to follow.

She ran clear of the trailers toward the longer grass
by the riverbank. Blackie looked back and gave a short,
sharp bark. He stood, ears pricked, hackles raised
down the length of his spine. "What is it?" She ran up to
him. He crouched down and barked again, ran two or
three steps, then returned.

"Show me, Blackie! Go on, boy!" Mandy whispered.
She followed the dog down the bank onto the narrow
pebble beach. And there was Vicki, crouching behind a

tree branch that swept low over the water. She looked wretched and afraid.

"Keep him off me, Mandy! Don't let him bite!" she pleaded. Heavy strands of hair had fallen over her eyes, but Mandy could see how miserable she looked behind the tumbled locks. She gripped the bough until her knuckles turned white.

Mandy stared. "It's all right, he won't hurt you," she said. She stretched out both her hands and spoke carefully. "Vicki, for heaven's sake, give Henry to me!"

Tears began to roll down the girl's face. "I can't." She trembled and hid her face behind her hands. "I haven't got him!"

Mandy groaned. She heard Brandon and James running through the long grass. They came to a halt just a few yards behind. "You must, Vicki. Your aunt told us that you have him. Now just hand him over, please!" She felt her nerves stretch to their limit. Her own hands were trembling.

"No, honestly, I haven't got him anymore!" She looked up and sniffed, trying to pull herself together. "But it's all right, don't worry. Everything's going to be fine!"

Bewildered, Mandy glanced the length of the beach. "What do you mean? Where is he? What have you done with Henry, Vicki?"

"Listen, I want to tell you the whole thing!" Vicki took a step forward. "Tell him to sit, James." She waited while Blackie obeyed his owner's command. Then she came up close to Mandy. "All this happened because I was jealous," she began. "When James was allowed to bring Henry home for the summer, I didn't think it was fair!"

Mandy clearly remembered Vicki's mutterings and dark looks, but she was impatient. "Vicki, we don't have time for this! Just tell us where Henry is now!"

"I will, Mandy. But first, I want you to listen. You have to understand, then you can tell everyone what happened. I don't want them to hate me after all this!"

Though Vicki was tall and easily able to take care of herself, something about the way she talked got through to Mandy. "Look, it's okay. If we get Henry back safe and sound, none of this will matter," Mandy assured her.

"Well, he's all right. You've got to believe me!"

Mandy nodded. "Go on, then."

"It's just that I've always wanted to take Henry home, see. And when James was the one who was chosen, I just thought it was so unfair. James and you have loads of animals to look after already.

"Anyway, I sat around at home moping and getting on

Justin's nerves. Then when we came to stay in Welford with my aunt, he had an idea!" By now, Vicki was so eager to tell her version of events that she forgot all about her fear of Blackie. She laid one hand on Mandy's arm. "We were busy keeping out of trouble after Antonia knocked over those flowerpots. There isn't much to do in Welford, just hang around, you know. Then Justin had this idea! 'Let's kidnap Henry, if you're so eager to look after him!' he said. He thought it would stop me from moaning and give us something to do.

"His other idea was to make it look like the kids from Riverside were the ones to blame again. He said it worked pretty well before. I asked how and he said, 'Easy as pie. We'll go over to James's place and make a bit of a mess of his yard, make it look like vandals have been at it again. Then all you have to do is steal Henry from his cage!' He said no one would ever know it was us!"

"And you went along with it?" Mandy stared at her, openmouthed.

Vicki's lip trembled and she nodded. "I just wanted to look after Henry!" she whispered.

James came and broke into the amazed silence. "Go on, Vicki. Never mind the yard. Just tell us what happened next."

"Well, the thing is, Justin went a bit crazy. He trampled everywhere, I couldn't stop him. He said he had to make it look like the Riverside kids had been at it again." The tears rose again as she looked at James. "I'm really sorry, James!"

He nodded. "Is that it? You wrecked the flowers and forced open Henry's cage?"

"No." Vicki took another deep breath. "It gets worse!"

"Go on, you might as well spit it out." Brandon climbed down the bank and offered his commonsense opinion. "Get it over and done with."

"It's about Leanne, isn't it?" Mandy took a guess. Somewhere in the middle of all this, she felt that Vicki would be able to explain Leanne's disappearance, too.

"How did you know?"

"Well, she's run away, and my guess is she didn't vanish for nothing. Go on, Vicki, tell us what happened next."

"I was just lifting Henry out of his cage. Justin broke open the bolt with a screwdriver he brought with him. I thought we were going to get clean away, but just then the gate swung open and it was Leanne walking up the path toward us. You should've seen her face, Mandy. It was like someone had shot her. She saw me holding Henry and she sort of gasped. She dropped a little bag of food she'd brought for him and she turned white as a sheet. She tried to grab Henry from me, but Justin got in the way and warned her to keep her mouth shut!"

Mandy pictured the scene; Leanne struggling to rescue Henry, Justin bullying. Two against one. No chance.

"Justin laughed at her. He said he'd put the blame on her when they found Henry missing! Everyone would know it was her because she was the one who was crazy about Henry. He said everyone hated her anyway!"

Mandy's eyebrows knitted together in a deep frown. "What did she do?"

"She kind of crumpled, then she ran off. I just stood there. Justin thought it was funny, and he went off as if nothing had happened." Vicki's voice trailed off at last.

"You know that Leanne hasn't been seen since, don't you?" James said quietly.

Miserably, Vicki nodded. Her lip quivered again. "I said I was sorry."

Mandy wasn't sure that "sorry" was enough. Leanne and Henry had both got the fright of their lives because of the twins, and they were both still missing. "But you told me Henry was okay, didn't you? So just take us to him now." She knew she sounded stiff and unfriendly, but right then she couldn't help it.

"Okay, I'll show you. Come on." Vicki led the way up

the bank and through the trailer park. "I did know that we'd done something really awful," she confessed. "When Justin showed up at Aunty's house, I said I wanted to take Henry straight back. That was after I'd had the chance to think about it. He was so mad. He said the plan had gone wrong in any case, and you'd found out the truth. I said I didn't care anymore. I just wanted to put Henry back in his cage. I never wanted any of this to happen!"

"Is that where Justin is now, at my house?" James asked. He had Blackie back on the leash as they broke into a run across the field.

"Yes. In the end he had to agree." Vicki began to gasp as she ran. "But he said he would be the one to take Henry back. I'd only mess things up if I went along. He told me to wait here while he did it. He promised no one would see him if he was by himself."

Mandy glanced at James. She didn't like the thought of Henry in Justin's tender care. "Is your mom home?" she asked.

James nodded.

"But Justin would be able to creep up without being seen, wouldn't he? He promised he would!" Vicki insisted.

"Let's hope." Brandon pulled up as he reached the

gate ahead of the others. He pointed across the road. "Here comes Justin now."

They heard Justin's heavy footsteps on the road. They saw him bend and shove something quickly into the hedge. They waited as he stood up and looked around. Then he spotted them. His face fell a mile. Mandy went to meet him.

"It's okay. Vicki's told us the whole thing," she said to him. "It doesn't matter, just as long as Henry's back where he belongs!" She longed for him to confirm it, that Henry was snug in his cage. Just those words, that was all.

He rocked back on his heels, scowling. He gave a short laugh. "Tough!" he said.

"What do you mean?" Vicki pushed forward. "Justin, you promised to put Henry back!"

"Too risky." He shrugged. "There was someone in the house. I couldn't get anywhere near without being spotted."

"What are you saying?" Mandy demanded. "Where's Henry? What have you done with him?" She still hoped against hope that Justin had taken the hamster back. "Where is he?"

"How should I know?"

"Why, what have you done with him?"

Justin blushed, but he hid his guilt with a final show of bravado. "Didn't you see? I just dumped him in the hedge back there." He jerked one thumb over his shoulder. "So what's wrong with that, then? I did him a favor, didn't I? No more running around on that old wheel for Henry. No more being locked up in a cage. I put him back in the wild. I set him free!"

Eleven

Terrified, Mandy ran along the road. Setting Henry "free" was like passing a death sentence. He would be in immediate danger from foxes, badgers, dogs, cats. Even the stress of being alone in a wide open space might be enough to kill him. She stooped to rummage through the undergrowth in the hedge bottom, hoping that he'd simply curled into a ball until they came to rescue him. But there was no sign.

"At least we know he's still in there somewhere," James said. "He couldn't have run out onto the road, or else we'd have seen him!"

She nodded. "Okay, let's all go back into the field and

spread out to look for him!" She turned to Vicki. "Will you help? We need as many people as possible. Henry won't last very long if we leave him to fend for himself!"

Vicki glanced at Justin, whose face was by now red with shame. He hung his head forward and shifted uneasily from foot to foot. "Yes, we'll help!" she said firmly. "It's the least we can do. Come on, Justin, you stand guard out here in the road. Let's get a move on!" And she led the little band of searchers back into the field.

They looked high and low. They searched under clumps of grass and inside hollows. They combed the field, they called his name. Brandon delved into his pockets and found cookie crumbs. They tried to tempt Henry out of his hiding place by scattering them along the hedgerow. All in vain.

Then they enlisted help, as some of the others drifted back to Riverside. The unsuccessful search for Leanne turned into a search for Henry; soon half the kids from Riverside were ferreting through the undergrowth, underneath trailers, and down the riverbank.

But by four o'clock, Mandy's hopes of finding the hamster were sinking low.

"He can't just vanish!" Vicki protested.

They gathered in a knot outside the clubhouse, Mandy,

James, Brandon, Justin, and Vicki, while the Riverside crowd kept on looking. Chrissie Searle had just turned up from the village shop with a basketful of rolls that she'd ordered for the barbecue. She reported that there was still no sign of Leanne.

"Let's think; what would Henry be most likely to do in a situation like this?" It was James who thought straight as usual.

"He'd build a nest!" Mandy said. "That's what he'd try to do. He'd look for dry grass, bits of sheep's wool, anything soft. He'd want a nice warm place, somewhere out of the wind." She tried to plot Henry's probable movements since Justin had dumped him in the hedge.

"Now, now, we mustn't stand around idly chatting!" A loud voice interrupted them. "Don't you know that the poor girl is still missing?" A bright yellow figure strode across the field toward them.

Mandy stifled a groan. "Leanne's not the only one, Mrs. Ponsonby." Quickly she told the newcomer about Henry.

"Well, let's not waste any more time!" Mrs. Ponsonby rose to the occasion with true wartime spirit. She rallied the troops. "Twins, you take Brandon with you and carry out a systematic search inside the trailers! Who's to say that Henry, like any sensible little hamster, hasn't taken refuge inside a nice warm sleeping bag or sock drawer?"

Eagerly Mandy nodded. "Yes, we haven't tried inside the trailers yet!"

So Brandon and the twins set off under Mrs. Ponsonby's command. Next she turned to Mandy, James, and Blackie, the light of determination glinting in her eyes. "And have you tried inside the store? Just the place for a hungry hamster, don't you think?"

She took a few steps toward the door. "Now, while you continue with the search in here, let me see how I can make myself more useful!" She rolled up the chiffon sleeves of her yellow dress, then turned to Chrissie Searle. "Chrissie, my dear, I take it that the basket contains provisions for tonight's barbecue?" Mrs. Ponsonby didn't pause for a reply. "Well, just carry it inside for me, would you, dear? My best plan is to continue with the food preparations, so that your little farewell party can go ahead according to schedule." She marched inside with an air of hope and certainty.

Mandy's eyes widened. "Do as she says!" she whispered. Chrissie picked up the basket and followed Mrs. Ponsonby into the clubroom, while James and Mandy turned into the store, stacked with cans, boxes of chips, shelves of cookies, and racks of fresh fruit.

"Isn't she amazing?" Chrissie said, once she'd deposited the basket with Mrs. Ponsonby, who immediately set to work with the bread knife. She sliced through the rolls with surgical precision. "How can she be so sure we'll have anything to celebrate?"

"I don't know, but don't argue," Mandy whispered. She dived behind the store counter on her hands and knees, calling out Henry's name. Mrs. Ponsonby had an eye on them through the open doorway. "What are you going to do now?" Mandy asked Chrissie.

"Find Pete and keep on looking for Leanne. It may be time we got the police involved." She looked serious as she went out and strode across the field.

Mrs. Ponsonby had injected fresh energy into both searches. James stood on a chair to investigate the high shelves, while Mandy covered every square inch of the store at ground level. Outside, the Riverside crowd still raked through the grass, while Vicki, Justin, and Brandon kept on examining the trailers. But still there was no sign of Henry or Leanne.

Swish went the blade of Mrs. Ponsonby's knife, chopping down onto the cutting board. She used the pool table covered with a sheet of thick plastic as a temporary surface. The rolls piled high on the table as she lifted each one from the basket to dissect it.

Swish — chop — pause. Swish — chop — pause.

"Henry!" Mandy called softly, trying to entice him out of hiding, crawling on all fours.

"Not up here," James sighed. He climbed down from the chair.

"Aagh!" A scream rang out from Mrs. Ponsonby. She snatched her hand away from the basket, and she dropped her knife and jumped a mile. "Oh, my, oh, my! There's a rat!" She backed against the pool table. "In the basket! A rat! Oh, my, don't let it get out!"

Mandy and James sprang through the door into the clubroom. They spotted stout Mrs. Ponsonby cowering against the table, her face and neck mottled red, her hands clasped in front of her chest. Together they dived for the basket. They peered inside.

"It's not a rat; it's Henry!' James said calmly.

Mandy cried out in delight. "Henry!" Unmistakably him, with his cheeks full of bread crumbs, his thick golden coat dusted with flour, his eyes twinkling.

"No, no, it's a rat, a rodent! In the basket! I'm sure it's a rat!" Mrs. Ponsonby's chins quivered. Her wartime spirit had evaporated.

"No, look," James explained, as Mandy gently lifted Henry from the basket to cradle him in her hands. "It's a hamster. He has no tail, see. And rats are gray. Henry's golden brown." He examined Henry's pudgy cheeks.

"And he's just gone and ruined his diet all over again!" he declared.

Mrs. Ponsonby peered more closely. "Hmm." She sounded doubtful. "I'm not up on the anatomy of rodents," she admitted. There was a pause. "Perhaps you are right."

"Oh, we are. It's Henry!" Relief brought tears to Mandy's eyes. "You were right, Mrs. Ponsonby! Henry did the sensible thing and headed for cover. He must have crept into Chrissie's basket when she left it outside on the grass. Trust Henry to head for food!"

Sure now of Henry's status as adorable pet, Mrs. Ponsonby moved in to study him. "He certainly is a charming little fellow," she agreed. "Here, Mandy, give him to me. Let me have a good look!"

Mandy took a deep breath. She could hardly refuse, she decided. Carefully she handed Henry over. "Hold him gently under the tummy," she said. "Cup your hands a little bit more . . . oh!"

"*Oh!*" Mrs. Ponsonby gave a little yelp and a shiver. "He tickles!" She opened her fingers and flattened her palms, then took her hands away with a sudden jerk.

Henry dropped onto the table, landed on all fours, and took a surprised look around. Then he scrambled down the nearest table leg.

"Watch out!" James ran to close the door. Henry scuttled across the floor. He sniffed and twitched this way and that, zigzagging across the room.

"Got him!" Mandy cried. She almost cupped her hands over the top of him, but he darted sideways and vanished under the bottom of another, narrower door.

Mandy sagged forward in dismay.

"It's okay. I think it's some sort of storeroom or cupboard!" James seized the handle and turned it. "It's locked!"

"No, I saw it open a crack. Something must be caught on the inside!" Mandy was right behind him, adding her weight. They pulled at the door with all their might.

There was a small cry as the door gave way. Someone stepped out of the storeroom. It was Leanne. She stared at them, her face pale, her green eyes wide with fright, her red hair tumbling around her cheeks. Safe between her trembling hands she held Henry.

The full story came out in the clubroom at Riverside. The search parties gathered happily, compared notes, and congratulated one another. Apologies flew from villager to visitor. News went around that everyone was safe.

"And we're ready for the barbecue!" Mrs. Ponsonby announced. She took full credit for assisting in Henry and Leanne's rescue. "It was nothing!" she murmured. "Really, nothing at all!"

Mandy grinned at James. "It's mostly Blackie we should thank!" she whispered. "Without him, we'd never have gotten onto Justin's track in the first place!"

James had delivered Henry and Blackie safely back home. While his dad fitted a new lock to the cage, James had weighed him. He was definitely a bit heavier but content. The hamster was now fast asleep after his long adventure.

Mrs. Ponsonby reveled in the happy ending. She reminded them once more of the barbecue, then pointed to an approaching figure. "But wait, here comes Mr. Western! Why, Sam, surely you've heard the good news?"

Sam Western stopped in the midst of the happy group. He was not a comfortable man. He cleared his throat. "That's a matter of opinion," he mumbled.

"Oh, come now, we've admitted our mistake. Mr. Parker Smythe has telephoned the leader of the council to give his support to the trailer site. Let bygones be bygones, eh?"

Mandy saw Mr. Western swallow hard. "That may be. But I thought it only right to come and tell you another bit of 'good' news." He surveyed his eager audience.

"I've just been speaking to my farm manager, Dennis Saville, and it seems one of my men has come to him with a confession. He told Dennis he took a Land Rover for a spin earlier this week, without asking permission. He brought it across country, down to the river . . ." There was a pause.

"Speak up, Sam Western!" Ernie Bell's voice growled from the back of the crowd. Half the village had congregated in the field.

"Well, the man's a novice behind the wheel. And, to cut a long story short, he knocked into a couple of trees by the tennis courts. That's it!" He finished abruptly, overcome with embarrassment.

There was another pause. Then someone cheered. Soon everyone was smiling and shouting and shaking hands.

"And I'll tell you something else." Ernie sidled up to Mandy. "Walter's got his geraniums back."

She thought he meant there'd been a miracle. "That's fantastic!"

"Not the *same* geraniums, you understand," Ernie said. "No, Walter's got new pots and new geraniums. Pretty as a picture, they look, standing on his front wall!"

"Where from?"

"From Mrs. Platt. She thought it was only neighborly,

so she drove over to Walton earlier this afternoon and bought some fine new plants. She says the twins must pay for them out of their allowance."

Mandy nodded thoughtfully. "You know, Vicki was really sorry in the end. And I think Justin was, too, deep down." She looked around, but they'd left the field.

"Yes, well, they'll feel it in their pockets, and that's no bad thing, I say." Ernie ambled off, saying that he might come back for the barbecue. "Just to see what it's like, mind," he growled. "I'm not one for newfangled ideas like open-air cooking, but I might just stick my nose in and take a look!"

The glowing faces around the barbecue that evening were proof of how well things had turned out. The clouds had cleared away, a full moon shone down.

Imogen came along with her mom and dad. James was there with Blackie. Brandon came early with his little brother and sister. The McFarlanes brought a free jar of candy, the Hardys came from the pub with soft drinks. Bert Burnley, the farmer, had good news from the council leader. "The trailers stay here at Riverside for the rest of the summer!" he announced. Adam Hope hugged Emily and led the chorus of cheers.

Mandy stood between her mom and dad, her face aching with so much smiling. Grandma and Grandpa were there to join the celebrations. The whole village was united again. And there was Mrs. Ponsonby, the "heroine" of the day, describing for the umpteenth time the part she had played in the rescue of Leanne and Henry.

"The poor girl had no one to turn to," she explained to Walter Pickard. "So she just hid away in the clubhouse, too miserable to come out. Apparently, she was absolutely convinced that she would get the blame for the hamster's disappearance! And then when I went in there to make sandwiches, she squeezed herself into that tiny storeroom, poor child, still hoping to avoid discovery!"

Mandy listened. "Just a second." She grinned at her parents. "I have an idea!"

Adam Hope took a deep breath. "Be warned!" he told the others.

Mandy sped across the grass to Mrs. Ponsonby's side. "There's only one thing I still feel sorry about," she dropped in casually. She stared up at the starlit sky.

"Oh, what's that?" Mrs. Ponsonby couldn't see any dents in the perfect conclusion.

"It's poor Leanne. She has to go home tomorrow, back to Birmingham. She can't keep pets where she lives. But she loves animals, she really does!"

"Hmm." Mrs. Ponsonby looked thoughtful.

Mandy rushed on. "Of course, their school could keep a pet, couldn't it? I mean, Kingsmill would be able to have a hamster in their biology lab, just like Walton." She sighed. "I expect that's the closest Leanne could get to having her own pet. Only I don't think Kingsmill has one at present . . ." She allowed her voice to trail off.

"Hmm." By now, Mrs. Ponsonby's thoughts were racing ahead. "Would you excuse me, Mandy, my dear? Now, where's that nice child with the blond hair? Sonia, isn't it? Ah, Sonia, there you are! Just a minute, my dear, may I have a word with you?" And she trotted off.

Mandy grinned. Her stomach bubbled with excitement. It was her last wish for the evening, her parting gift for Leanne.

The Kingsmill School minibus stood at the gate, ready to depart. It was eleven o'clock on Saturday morning. The roof rack was piled high with backpacks, all covered and tied down under a tarpaulin. The kids were piling onto the bus, while Mandy stood with James, who carried Henry inside his cage for a last farewell.

"Bye!" Mandy shouted. Ben gave her a thumbs-up sign as he parked himself on the backseat. Marcie waved both hands and grinned. Sonia climbed in next. She grinned over her shoulder at Mandy. "I suppose the countryside wasn't so bad after all!" She laughed. Then

Paul climbed on, with his soccer ball tucked safely under one arm. And just as Leanne came to say good-bye to Mandy, James, and Henry, Mrs. Ponsonby drove her car into the field.

Mandy held her breath. Mrs. Ponsonby got out and opened the back of her car. She took a large, square object from the trunk. It was covered in a piece of light white fabric. Grandly, she carried it toward Leanne.

"Now, before you say anything about this, I've checked with your principal on the telephone, and she's perfectly willing for the school to take Elizabeth. And she promised to phone your mother, and your mother has agreed. So, no worry on that score!" She held out the box for Leanne to take.

"Elizabeth?" Leanne frowned. She glanced at Mandy.

Mandy looked back, all wide-eyed innocence.

"Elizabeth the First," Mrs. Ponsonby explained. "Daughter of Henry the Eighth, you know. Most appropriate." With a smile and a final grand gesture, she whisked away the cloth.

A pretty cream-colored hamster with dark brown eyes nestled in the straw on the bottom of a wooden cage. Her eyes were huge and round, her ears neat and tufted. A band of white under her chin and around her neck shone clean and bright. She twitched her whiskers

and blinked, then came forward to the front of her cage to say hello.

"Elizabeth the First," Leanne repeated under her breath. She was mesmerized.

"I went over to Walton first thing this morning," Mrs. Ponsonby went on. "The man in the pet shop says she's a good-natured little creature, ideal for being with children." She paused and glanced toward the minibus. "There's only one teeny-weeny little problem." Everyone craned out of the window to take a look at the new Kingsmill hamster. "Who will take care of Elizabeth for the rest of the summer?"

Mandy thought she saw Mrs. Ponsonby wink. Leanne was too busy gazing at the hamster to notice.

"Leanne!" they shouted, without a shadow of a doubt.

"Leanne should keep her!"

"She knows all about hamsters!"

"She's the expert!"

Leanne blushed and smiled, and tears of happiness filled her eyes. "Thank you," she whispered to Mrs. Ponsonby.

Mrs. Ponsonby put one arm around her shoulder and squeezed it. "You should thank Mandy and James," she said gently.

"Thank you," Leanne managed to say. "For everything." She carried the cage onto the bus, and was surrounded by friends who all wanted a good view of the new school hamster.

"Thank you." Chrissie leaned out of the driver's seat and smiled at Mrs. Ponsonby. "That was very kind. And we'll be back on Monday with a new gang. See you then."

As the bus drove off, Mandy noticed Mrs. Ponsonby take a lace hankie from her handbag. She gave a genteel sniff and dabbed her eyes.

"Say good-bye, Henry!" Mandy said. She waved them out of sight.

But Henry, back on his diet of lettuce leaves and dried oats, was hard at work on his exercise wheel. It rattled steadily as James and Mandy carried him down to the river, kicked off their shoes, and stuck their feet in the cool, clear water. Mandy lifted Henry out of his cage and sat him on her lap in the full sunlight. He fidgeted, then curled up to sleep. She stroked him softly and began to daydream. The bright river flowed by. Henry snored. She was completely happy.

PONY PALS
Be a Pony Pal!

☐ BBC 0-590-48583-0	#1	I Want a Pony	....	$3.99 US
☐ BBC 0-590-48584-9	#2	A Pony for Keeps	....	$3.99 US
☐ BBC 0-590-48585-7	#3	A Pony in Trouble	....	$3.99 US
☐ BBC 0-590-48586-5	#4	Give Me Back My Pony	....	$3.99 US
☐ BBC 0-590-25244-5	#5	Pony to the Rescue	....	$3.99 US
☐ BBC 0-590-25245-3	#6	Too Many Ponies	....	$3.99 US
☐ BBC 0-590-54338-5	#7	Runaway Pony	....	$3.99 US
☐ BBC 0-590-54339-3	#8	Good-bye Pony	....	$3.99 US
☐ BBC 0-590-62974-3	#9	The Wild Pony	....	$3.99 US
☐ BBC 0-590-62975-1	#10	Don't Hurt My Pony	....	$3.99 US
☐ BBC 0-590-86597-8	#11	Circus Pony	....	$3.99 US
☐ BBC 0-590-86598-6	#12	Keep Out, Pony!	....	$3.99 US
☐ BBC 0-590-86600-1	#13	The Girl Who Hated Ponies	....	$3.99 US
☐ BBC 0-590-86601-X	#14	Pony-Sitters	....	$3.99 US
☐ BBC 0-590-86632-X	#15	The Blind Pony	....	$3.99 US
☐ BBC 0-590-37459-1	#16	The Missing Pony Pal	....	$3.99 US
☐ BBC 0-590-37460-5	#17	Detective Pony	....	$3.99 US
☐ BBC 0-590-51295-1	#18	The Saddest Pony	....	$3.99 US
☐ BBC 0-590-63397-X	#19	Moving Pony	....	$3.99 US
☐ BBC 0-590-63401-1	#20	Stolen Ponies	....	$3.99 US
☐ BBC 0-590-63405-4	#21	The Winning Pony	....	$3.99 US
☐ BBC 0-439-06488-0	#22	The Western Pony	....	$3.99 US
☐ BBC 0-439-06489-9	#23	The Pony and the Bear	....	$3.99 US
☐ BBC 0-439-06490-2	#24	The Unlucky Pony	....	$3.99 US
☐ BBC 0-439-06491-0	#25	The Lonely Pony	....	$3.99 US
☐ BBC 0-590-74210-8		Pony Pals Super Special #1: The Baby Pony	......	$5.99 US
☐ BBC 0-590-86631-1		Pony Pals Super Special #2: The Lives of our Ponies	..	$5.99 US
☐ BBC 0-590-37461-3		Pony Pals Super Special #3: The Ghost Pony	......	$5.99 US

Available wherever you buy books, or use this order form.

Send orders to Scholastic Inc., P.O. Box 7500, Jefferson City, MO 65102

Please send me the books I have checked above. I am enclosing $_____ (please add $2.00 to cover shipping and handling). Send check or money order — no cash or C.O.D.s please.

Please allow four to six weeks for delivery. Offer good in the U.S.A. only. Sorry, mail orders are not available to residents of Canada. Prices subject to change.

Name_____ Birthdate _____/_____/_____
     First   Last   M   D   Y

Address_____

City_____ State_____ Zip_____

Telephone (_____) _____ ☐ Boy   ☐ Girl

Where did you buy this book?   ☐ Bookstore   ☐ Book Fair   ☐ Book Club   ☐ Other   PP1099

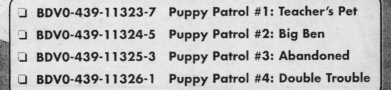